THE ANTHOLOGY OF
SCOTTISH
FOLK TALES

Dedicated by Scotland's Storytellers

TO
LAWRENCE TULLOCH
1943- 2017

We'll tak a cup of kindness yet
For auld lang syne

First published 2019
Reprinted 2021

The History Press
97 St George's Place, Cheltenham,
Gloucestershire, GL50 3QB
www.thehistorypress.co.uk

British Library Cataloguing in Publication Data.
A catalogue record for this book is available from the British Library.

ISBN 978 0 7509 9203 9

Typesetting and origination by The History Press
Printed by TJ Books Limited, Padstow, Cornwall

FOREWORD

Why is Scotland such fertile folk tale territory?

First of all, Scotland is a very diverse country, geographically and culturally. It is big and wee at the same time. It is part of Great Britain yet proudly independent in identity and imagination. From Shetland and Orkney in the north, to the Borders and Dumfries and Galloway in the south; from the Western Isles to Aberdeenshire and Fife in the east, landscapes and language vary, sometimes dramatically. In the Highlands, sea and mountain predominate, while in Perthshire it is river and glen.

Secondly, this is a living tradition. These tales have not been excavated from dusty tomes. All the contributors are current storytellers as we go to press, with the sad exception of Lawrence Tulloch who died in 2017. We are all honoured to be dedicating this book to that most generous host and inspirer of Scotland's contemporary storytelling renaissance.

But lastly, these stories matter because they bring us all closer to the natural world, to our shared centuries of human endeavour, and to sustaining values. Never has the world had so much need of such stories, and Scotland is proud to make its contribution. Here is a perfect introduction to Scotland, the storytelling nation – explore and enjoy.

Donald Smith
Director, Scottish International Storytelling Festival

CONTENTS

Western Isles
South Uist: Asking for the Wind p.34
Lewis and Outlying Islands:
Who Was Chasing Who? p.39

The Highlands
The Seal Killer p.44
A Highland Origin Myth p.48

Argyll
The Song of the Wind p.84
The Harper of Lochbuie p.92

Scottish Borders
Thomas the Rhymer p.134
The Laddie that Kept Hares p.141

Dumfries and Galloway
The Milk White Doo p.152
The Puddock p.167

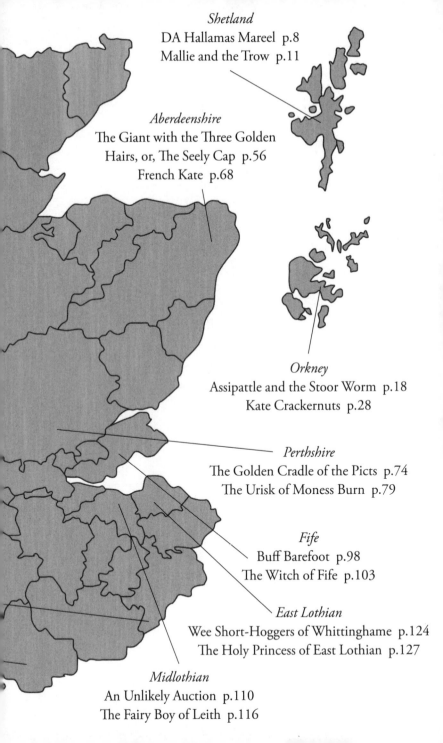

Shetland
DA Hallamas Mareel p.8
Mallie and the Trow p.11

Aberdeenshire
The Giant with the Three Golden
Hairs, or, The Seely Cap p.56
French Kate p.68

Orkney
Assipattle and the Stoor Worm p.18
Kate Crackernuts p.28

Perthshire
The Golden Cradle of the Picts p.74
The Urisk of Moness Burn p.79

Fife
Buff Barefoot p.98
The Witch of Fife p.103

East Lothian
Wee Short-Hoggers of Whittinghame p.124
The Holy Princess of East Lothian p.127

Midlothian
An Unlikely Auction p.110
The Fairy Boy of Leith p.116

SHETLAND

LAWRENCE TULLOCH

LAWRENCE TULLOCH was born in North Yell in 1942 and was introduced to storytelling by his aunt and his father. His interest in folklore led to him making several radio broadcasts, and he wrote for magazines and local papers. He had four books published and left two written but not published when he sadly passed away in February 2017.

As a storyteller he travelled extensively: to Washington USA, the Faroe Islands, Sweden, Norway, Slovenia, Ireland and Orkney, and he participated in several Scottish festivals including the International Storytelling Festival in Edinburgh and Celtic Connections in Glasgow. He recorded two tapes of stories and had them remastered to CDs.

He enjoyed telling stories and loved the audience reaction, which always left a twinkle in his eye.

DA HALLAMAS MAREEL

At the Burgi Geo in northwest Yell there lies the remains of an Iron Age fort. It is on a headland joined to the rest of the island by a narrow neck of land. There are rows of standing stones that lead, on one side, into the fort, but on the other side the standing stones lead the unwary over the high cliff and to their doom.

Long after the original inhabitants left, the fort was taken over by a ruthless and cruel band of Vikings who preyed on the honest and hardworking udallers: West-A-Firth, in those days, was a wild and lawless place.

It was late autumn and the children of West-A-Firth were preparing for Hallamas. Wearing the traditional straw hats, they had been to every house in the area collecting money the taditional party that took place every year. All the houses that is, save one. It was a miserable hovel deep in the hills, where the Spaeman, the hermit Isaac Omand, lived. He welcomed no one and no one knew how he made a living. If he was ever heard speaking it was always in riddles that no one could understand.

All the money collected for Hallamas was given to Mary. She was a spinster who lived alone but she loved children and she was always to the fore at Hallamas time. Along with Martha Rassusson and Jenny Ninian she went to the shop at Glippapund to buy the food for the party.

For the rest of the week they baked fatty bannocks, currney buns, oven sliddericks and dumplings. They made tattie soup they kirned for fresh butter, kirn milk and blaand. A lamb had been butchered and meat and mealy puddings were cooked.

When Mary returned home after visiting a neighbour she was distraught to find that the robbers from the Burgi Geo had raided the house and taken everything. On being told, the Oldest Udaller called a meeting and the folk came from Setter, the Neap, Graven and Vigon to discuss what they could do.

There was no question of confronting the Vikings; they were far too powerful and to try and fight them meant the certain loss of life. Sadly there were no suggestions and most were resigned to their fate.

'Der only da wan thing we kan dü,' declared the Oldest Udaller, 'we maun geng an ax the Spaeman.'

'Der nae öse o dat,' said Sigurd Ollason, 'he'll never spik tae wis an even if he dus we'll nivver keen whit he means.'

In the absence of any other ideas, Sigurd and Tirval Ertirson were sent to consult the Spaeman. When they arrived at his house they got the impression that Isaac Omand was expecting them.

He was outside, a tiny man dressed in rags; he had a long grey beard and he had not washed for a very long time. He never gave them a chance to speak but said in a shrill wavering voice:

> Da Burgi Geo men ir fat an greedy
> While wis puir fok ir tin an needy
> Bit ta mak things rite an weel
> Ye maun öse da Hallamas mareel.

So saying, he went inside and shut the door leaving Sigurd and Tirval speechless. Feeling that their journey had been wasted, they made their way back to the house of the Oldest Udaller. They told him the Spaeman's rhyme and waited for his response, which took some time in coming.

'Da only plis it we kan get mareel fae is da sea so sum o you il haeta geng ta da kraigs.'

They saw it as futile but they did as they were told. They took their homemade rods and began fishing from the rocks. When the light began to fade they were astonished at the mareel in the water. They had never seen anything like it: the sea, the fish and the fishing line flashed with ribbons of fire.

On the way home Sigurd suddenly had an idea of how they could use the mareel. He was confident that the robbers would come to steal the fish so he got Tirval and others to skin the piltocks and sillocks. From the women-folk he got old blankets and pieces of linen and they began to sew the fish skins onto the cloth.

Six men donned the mareel-covered cloth and they set off westwards towards the Burgi Geo but hid below the banks of the burn to keep watch for the robbers. The mareel flashed like green fire in the moonlight.

They did not have to wait long and all the men kept low until Sigurd gave the shout and they all leaped up shouting, jumping and waving their arms. The effect on the robbers was amazing, they were terrified and turned tail and ran back towards the Burgi Geo as fast as they could go.

The West-A-Firth men followed, screaming and shouting. The robbers, in their panic, followed the wrong set of standing stones and every last one of them disappeared over the cliff to their death.

In the days that followed, the West-A-Firth men ventured into the fort and found it empty of people, but they were able to recover many of the things that the robbers had stolen from them over the years. And so the community enjoyed the best ever Hallamas and they were able to live in peace and with plenty ever after.

MALLIE AND THE TROW

Mallie was a widow who lived with her three sons. They were all big healthy young men, and their mother found it very hard to feed them. They were very poor; money was in short supply since the man of the house had been lost at sea.

At the start of every winter they had a few potatoes, a small barrel of salted herrings and a boll (140lbs) of oatmeal. As the boys got bigger, Mallie found it harder and harder to make this scanty supply of food last all winter.

There came the time, the winter still had a distance to go, when the last of the herring was taken from the barrel and the last of the meal was taken from the girner. As they ate this frugal meal Mallie explained that they had no more food left and hungry days lay ahead.

The following day the boys were all as hungry as ever and there was no food.

'What are we going to do?' asked the oldest son.

'We shall have to become beggars, there is nothing else for it,' he was told.

The old woman who lived close by always seemed to have plenty of food, so the same boy volunteered to go and ask her. He knocked on her door and she came and answered it.

'All our food has been eaten, we are all going hungry, please can you give us something to eat?'

He could see into the kitchen of the house, he could see that the cupboard door was open and the shelves were laden with food. There was bread, cheese, cooked meat, oatmeal, flour, tea, coffee and jar after jar of jam and preserves; the cupboard was filled to overflowing.

The old woman gave the boy a withering look.

'Go away, how dare to come to my door begging, I have nothing to give you and do not come back or it will be worse for you.'

He came back home to his mother and his brothers, crying. He was a big boy and crying was for babies but he was so hungry and he could not understand how that woman could be so hard and unkind.

'Some folk are like that, son,' his mother said. 'Be pleased that we are different.'

Late in the afternoon a knock came to the door and standing on the doorstep was a little old man with grey hair and twinkling blue eyes but dressed in rags.

'Can you give me something to eat?' he asked. 'I have been on the road for two days without any food at all.'

Mallie explained to him that they had no food either but he was welcome to come in and warm himself by the fire. The old man thanked her and came into the kitchen. After he had settled down and was speaking to the boys, Mallie went to the herring barrel.

There were no herring in it, she knew that, but there was some brine. She went to the meal girner and, using a small brush made from the grass that grew near the shore, she swept the corners of the box, the lid and the bottom.

Mallie was surprised at how much she got from the girner, she took it and mixed it with the brine. It was enough that everyone got a small amount in a cup but Mallie had hardly any for herself.

The old man sat by the fire and asked if he could stay with them overnight.

'We have no bed for you but you are welcome to stay by the fire. We have plenty of peats so at least you can be warm,' Mallie replied.

The following morning one of the boys went to the well for a bucket of water and each of them had a drink. The old man took his departure and he thanked the family for their hospitality.

They all said goodbye and the old man walked away. The boys had gone back indoors and Mallie was about to turn in and shut the door when the man turned back and spoke again to Mallie.

'That meal and brine that we had last night, was that really the very last of your food?' he asked. Mallie told him that it was the last and she had no idea what they would have from now on. The old man considered for a time and then said, 'It is a very special person who will share the very last that they have.'

With that he turned and walked away. Inside there was a gloom settling over the house. Mallie hated to see the boys so hungry and they were trying very hard not to complain. The fire burned down low and one of the boys went to the stack for a basketful of peats. At least they could be warm, he thought. When he came back, Mallie stoked up the fire. The peats were quite big and Mallie broke one in two. Something fell from the peat and tinkled on the floor.

When Mallie picked it up she saw that it was a gold coin. She broke another peat and out came another gold coin. Every peat proved to have a gold coin inside it and Mallie knew that the old man that visited was a trow and this was his way of saying thanks.

There was no more hunger for Mallie and the boys; they could buy anything they wanted. This did not go unnoticed; the old woman who refused to help them was curious to know where Mallie's money came from.

She spied on the family and saw Mallie breaking peats and picking up the coins. The woman waited until after dark and stole peats from Mallie's peat stack. She was not content with a basketful, so she took several and brought them into her kitchen.

However, when she broke a peat no coin appeared. Instead a mouse dropped to the floor and scuttled away looking for a place to hide. She broke open another and another as she looked in vain for gold coins, but all she got was more and more mice.

The mice multiplied like mad and soon the house was overrun with them. They got into her larder and they devoured every morsel of food that she had. In no time she had nothing to eat; the mice had consumed everything.

She endured two days of hunger and misery before she was reduced to begging. She knew that Mallie now had plenty so she came to Mallie's door and was greeted by the same boy that she had turned away from her own door.

The old woman told him that mice had overrun her home, she had no food, she was very hungry and could they please give her something.

'I will give you exactly the same as you gave me when we had nothing,' he told her, and slammed the door in her face.

Mallie asked him who he had been speaking to.

'It was that old woman from next door,' he said. 'She has the cheek to ask us for food and I have not forgotten how she treated me when I asked her for food.'

'Have you forgotten what I told you?' Mallie asked him. 'I told you that we were not like her.'

She opened the door and called the old woman back.

'Come in,' she said. 'Come in and sit by the fire and you can share the food that I am cooking. As long as we have any food you shall never go hungry.'

ORKNEY

TOM MUIR

Tom Muir tells stories from his native Orkney Islands, and has travelled the world, from the Arctic's North West Passage to the shores of the South China Seas and many countries in between. He has published books on Orkney folk tales, making these stories accessible to everyone so that they will continue to be retold. It has been his lifelong work to save Orkney's stories for future generations.

He and his his wife Rhonda have created the website Orkneyology.com, and teamed up with Robert Gordon University to create a free 'Orkney Folklore Trail' app, telling folk tales in the landscape. Tom works as Engagement/ Exhibitions Officer at the Orkney Museum.

ASSIPATTLE AND THE STOOR WORM

There was once a farmer who lived on a fine farm called Leegarth, which lay in a valley by the side of a stream. The farmer had a wife and seven sons, and they all worked hard on the farm. Well, that's not strictly true, you see, the parents and six elder sons worked hard, but the youngest son did nothing but lie beside the fire, raking through the ashes, so they called him Assipattle, which means ash raker. Assipattle regularly became covered with ashes and when he went out the ash would blow from him like smoke from a bonfire. The boy was also a great storyteller although in his stories he was always the hero who killed the dragon and married the princess. His brothers hated him and they would kick him on their way out the door, while his parents would just shake their heads sadly when they looked at him.

Now, one day a terrible thing happened; the Stoor Worm arrived at the land where Assipattle lived. This was no ordinary stoor worm, but the Mester Stoor Worm, the oldest, biggest and baddest stoor worm in the sea. A sea monster so big that it was wrapped right around the world, and when it moved it caused earthquakes and tidal waves. It could crush the mightiest ship between the forks of its tongue, or sweep whole villages into its mouth, and if that wasn't bad enough, its breath was poisonous and would kill any living thing it touched. What was worse, it was now lying off the coast of the land where Assipattle lived and it had started to yawn. This was a bad sign because it didn't mean that the Stoor Worm was tired, it meant that it was hungry and it wanted to be fed.

The king gathered together all his advisers and asked them what could be done. No one had any idea, but one of them, who was slightly smarter than the rest, suggested that they ask the Spaeman who lived on the side of the mountain. A spaeman is a wizard, and this one was the cleverest man in all the kingdom. He had a long white beard and carried a staff in his hand.

He gave the problem much thought before speaking, saying: 'Your Majesty, the Stoor Worm has travelled all over the world and eaten all sorts of exotic people, but now it is old and has developed a bit of a sweet tooth. If you were to feed it seven maidens for its breakfast every Saturday morning, then it would spare the rest of the kingdom.'

So, every Saturday morning seven maidens were bound hand and foot and placed on a flat rock in front of the Stoor Worm's head. When it woke, it yawned seven great yawns and then flicked out its tongue and picked the girls up, one by one, between the forks of its tongue, gobbling them up like sweeties.

One Saturday morning, Assipattle and his family went to see the Stoor Worm eat his terrible breakfast. The old man went white.

'There will soon be no more girls left in this land,' he cried, 'and I have seven sons. Who will they marry? Who will look after us in our old age if there are no more children?'

'Don't worry,' said Assipattle, 'I'll fight the Stoor Worm, and kill it!'

His brothers laughed and threw stones at him until he ran away.

That evening his mother told Assipattle to go to the barn where his brothers were threshing corn and tell them to come in for their supper. Assipattle went to the barn calling, 'Eh, boys; supper's ready.'

'Get him!' shouted his eldest brother, and they all jumped on top of him and covered him with straw.

They would have smothered him if their father hadn't gone out to see what was going on. He wasn't very happy, because it's kind of bad form to try to kill your brother. He gave them a smack on the lug as they went past him and he sent them to the house. He was still scolding them later at the table, but Assipattle said, 'It's all right father, if you hadn't come in when you did I was just about to give them all a damned good thrashing!'

'Well, why didn't you?' sneered his eldest brother.

'Because I'm saving my strength.'

'You? Saving your strength?' Laughed his brother. 'What are you saving your strength for?'

'For when I fight the Stoor Worm, of course!' said Assipattle.

His father shook his head and said, 'You'll fight the Stoor Worm when I make spoons from the horns of the moon!'

Time passed, and more maidens were fed to the Stoor Worm. Soon the people complained that this couldn't be allowed to carry on. The king called the Spaeman back to his palace and asked him what could be done to get rid of the monster for once and for all.

'Well,' said the Spaeman, 'there is one thing that would satisfy the Stoor Worm, but it is too terrible to say.'

'Say it,' shouted the king, 'and that is an order!'

'Well,' said the Spaeman, 'if you were to feed it the most beautiful maiden in the land; your daughter, the

Princess Gem de Lovely, then it would go away and spare your kingdom.'

'No!' shouted the court officials. 'That is too high a price to pay.'

But the king raised his hand and said, 'No; it is only right that my daughter, my only child, descended from the god Odin and heir to my kingdom, should die so that her people can live. But, I crave one indulgence. Give me three weeks to find a hero who can fight and kill the Stoor Worm. If anyone can do that I will give him my magic sword, Sikkersnapper, my kingdom and my daughter's hand in marriage.'

A proclamation went throughout the land asking for a hero to fight the Stoor Worm. Thirty-six brave knights rode into town, but when the first dozen saw the size of the Stoor Worm they rode right through the town, out the other side of the town and away home again. The second dozen fainted, and had to be carried out on stretchers, boots first. The third dozen sank into a deep depression and skulked in the king's castle, drinking his beer and wine. The king looked at them and he was disgusted, because the blood of an older and nobler race ran through his veins!

'Bring me my sword, Sikkersnapper,' he ordered, 'and make ready a boat. Tomorrow at dawn I will fight the Stoor Worm, or die in the attempt.'

News of this spread like wildfire throughout the kingdom; the king was going to fight the Stoor Worm. At Leegarth Assipattle was lying by the side of the fire. He was listening to his parents who were lying in their bed, and they were arguing.

'So, the king is going to fight the Stoor Worm,' said Assipattle's father, 'we can take my horse Teetgong; he's the fastest horse in the land, you know.'

'Yeah!' snorted his wife, in a disapproving voice.

'What's up with you tonight?' asked Assipattle's father. 'You're in a very sour mood.'

'And so I might be,' retorted his wife.

'Why? What have I done now?' asked the poor old man.

'You are keeping secrets from me, and I don't like it!'

'Why? What secrets am I keeping? I don't have any secrets from you, my dear.'

'Well, that horse of yours.'

'Teetgong; fastest horse in the land, you know!'

'I know,' she snapped, 'but there's something that you do that makes that horse run so fast, and I want to know what it is.'

'But, my dear, I can't tell you that.'

'And why not?'

'Well – because – you see – it's a – kind of – a – secret.'

'Ah, ha!' said his wife, triumphantly. 'I thought as much! And if you have one secret then maybe you have others!'

'Oh, I don't have any secrets from you my dear.'

This went on for some time, and Assipattle was listening. After a while his father gave in and said, 'All right, I'll tell you the secret of Teetgong's speed. If I want him to stand still, I pat him on the left shoulder. If I want him to run fast, I pat him on the right shoulder, but if I want him to run as fast as the wind, I blow through a goose's thrapple (windpipe); I keep one in my coat pocket in case of emergencies.'

Once she had heard this she was contented and soon they were both fast asleep, snoring away merrily. Assipattle got up from the side of the fire and went over to where his father's coat was hanging. He took out the goose's thrapple and slipped silently outside and headed to the stable.

When Teetgong saw him he started to neigh, rear up and kick, because this was not his master who was coming, but Assipattle gave him a pat on the left shoulder and he stood still. Assipattle got up on his back and gave him a pat on the right shoulder and away he ran, giving a loud neigh as he went. The sound of this woke up his father and he shouted to his sons to get horses and to ride after him.

'Stop! Thief!' they cried, because they didn't know that it was Assipattle.

After a short time his father was catching up, and he shouted, 'Hi, hi, ho! Teetgong, whoa!'

Teetgong stopped dead in his tracks, but Assipattle pulled out the goose's thrapple from his pocket and blew through it.

PAARP!

As soon as Teetgong heard the sound that it made he pricked up his ears and shot over the horizon, like an arrow from a bow. The old man and his sons gave up and turned their horses towards home. Assipattle clung on to Teetgong, who was well named, as in Orkney a Teetgong is a sudden gust of wind, and this horse could run as fast as any wind.

Eventually they came to a hill and down below them they saw a wide bay, and in that bay there was a big black island. However, it wasn't an island; it was the Stoor Worm's head. Assipattle rode down to the bay where he found a small house and went inside. There he saw an old woman lying asleep in her box bed with her grey cat curled up at her feet. The fire had been 'rested' for the night. In those days is was considered to be very bad luck to let your fire go out, as the luck of the house could go with it, so the fire was kept smouldering by putting damp peats on top of it. In the morning you just put some dry peats on top, gave it a puff with the bellows and away it would go. Assipattle took an iron pot from the side of the fire and he picked up a glowing peat with the fire tongs and put it into the pot and then ran outside.

Down by the shore he saw the king's boat with a guard standing in it, and he was blue with cold.

'Hello,' said Assipattle, 'what like?'

'Cold!' grumbled the guard.

'Well, I'm just going to light a fire to boil some limpets for my breakfast; would you like to have a warm by my fire?'

'Better not,' said the guard, 'I can't leave my post or I'll get into trouble.'

'Better stay where you are then,' said Assipattle and he started to dig a hole, like he was making a hearth to shelter his fire in. Suddenly he started to shout, 'Gold! Gold! There's gold here!'

'Gold?' said the guard. 'Where?'

The guard jumped out of the boat and ran over to where Assipattle was, pushed him out of the way and started to dig in the ground like a dog. Assipattle picked up the pot with the peat in it, jumped into the king's boat, cast off the rope, hoisted the sail and was away across the bay before the guard knew what had happened. When he looked around he saw the king and his men arrive, just as the sun appeared over the horizon. As the first rays of the sun kissed the Stoor Worm's eyes it started to wake up and it gave the first of its seven great yawns. Assipattle positioned the boat alongside the monster's mouth so that when it yawned again the boat was carried into the Stoor Worm's mouth with the water that rushed inside and he went right down the Stoor Worm's throat. Down,

down, deeper and deeper inside the Stoor Worm went Assipattle and the boat.

Now, I don't suppose that you are familiar with the internal plumbing of a stoor worm, so I had better explain. There was a large tunnel that ran right through the Stoor Worm, but here and there were smaller tunnels running off the big one and some of the water ran this way, some that way, until the water got shallower and shallower and the boat grounded. The inside of the monster glowed with a green, phosphorescent light, so Assipattle could easily see where he was going. He grabbed the pot with the peat in it and jumped out of the boat. Leaving the boat behind he ran and he better ran until he found what he was looking for; the Stoor Worm's liver! Well, you know how much oil there is in a fish's liver, so imagine the amount of oil in the Stoor Worm's liver. It would be enough to solve our energy requirements forever. Assipattle took a knife from his belt with which he cut a hole in the Stoor Worm's liver. Into the hole he put the burning peat and he blew and he better blew until the oil spluttered into flames and then he ran back to his boat.

Meanwhile, back on the shore, the king was having a bad day. First he'd had to get up really early in order to fight the Stoor Worm and meet certain death (which would be enough to put me in a bad mood for the rest of the day) and then he arrived just in time to see some idiot steal his boat, sail across the bay and get swallowed by the Stoor Worm. Oh great! It just doesn't get any better than that, does it? As he stood by the shore, fuming with rage, one of his men said, 'Eh, Your Majesty, I've never seen the Stoor Worm do that before.'

'Do what?' snapped the king, looking the other way.

'Well, he's kind of – he's sort of – smoking.'

'Smoking?' shouted the king.

'Aye, well, look!'

And sure enough, when the king looked out over the bay he could see black smoke starting to billow out of the Stoor Worm's nose and out of its mouth. Now, the Stoor Worm started to feel sick and it spewed up all the water that was inside of it, which headed towards the shore as a huge wave. The king and his men, the old woman from the cottage with her cat and all the horses ran up the hillside to safety as the wave drew nearer, with Assipattle in his boat riding the crest of it. The boat was cast up high and dry right by the side of the king.

The thick, black smoke filled the sky and blocked out the sun, turning day into night. In its dying agony the Stoor Worm shot out its huge forked tongue so high that it caught hold of the moon. It would have pulled it from the sky, but the fork of its tongue slipped over the horn of the moon and it came back down to earth with a thundering crash, leaving a huge hole in the surface of the world. Water poured into the hole and it cut off the land of the Danes from Norway and Sweden. There it remains to this day as the Baltic Sea, and if you look at a map you can still see the great forks of the Stoor Worm's tongue.

The Stoor Worm's days were finally over. It rose its head up out of the sea in its dying agony and it came back down to earth with a crash, which knocked out a lot of its teeth. These teeth fell into the sea and there they remain as the Orkney Islands. The head rose again and crash! More teeth were knocked out and these became Shetland. A third time the head rose and fell with a crash and more teeth were knocked out to make the Faroe Islands. Then the Stoor Worm curled up into a great big lump and died, and there it still remains; only now we call it Iceland. The flames that you see shooting out of the mountains there and the boiling water gushing out of the ground is caused by the Stoor Worm's liver, which is still burning.

The king took Assipattle in his arms and called him his son. He strapped the sword Sikkersnapper to his side and said, 'My boy, my kingdom is yours, as is my daughter, if she will have you.'

The Princess Gem de Lovely came over and as soon as she saw Assipattle she fell in love with him, because he was actually a very handsome young man, under all the ashes. The two of them were soon married and they reigned over the kingdom for many years and if they are not dead, then they are living yet.

⁂

You could well believe that story to be true if you have visited all the places created from the Stoor Worm's teeth. Orkney must be its incisors, as the islands are fairly flat. Shetland is formed from its premolars, higher and rugged, while the mountainous Faroe Islands are its molars, huge islands rising sheer from the sea to jagged points.

KATE CRACKERNUTS

There was once a king who had a beautiful young daughter called Anne who was the apple of his eye. However, tragedy struck the family when Anne's mother, the queen, took ill and died. After a while the king married again, taking a widowed queen as his wife. This queen had a daughter called Kate, who was about the same age as Anne. Kate loved nothing more than cracking nuts and eating them, so she was called Kate Crackernuts. Although these two princesses were not related they loved each other like true sisters. The queen, on the other hand, was jealous of Anne as she was more beautiful than her own daughter and she decided that she would find a way to spoil her lovely looks. She paid a visit to the hen wife who lived in a little tumbled-down cottage in the woods and kept the castle supplied with eggs. The hen wife was a black-hearted witch and she plotted with the queen to curse young Anne and rob her of her beauty.

'Send her to me tomorrow morning first thing,' said the hen wife, 'and make sure that she is fasting.'

The next morning the queen got Anne up early and told her to go to the hen wife to collect eggs. She got up, dressed, took a basket and went down the back stairs. As she was passing the kitchen she saw a piece of bread and so she took it and ate it on the road. When she reached the hen wife's cottage she knocked at the door and heard a voice telling her to come in. She opened the door and saw in the inky blackness inside that there was a pot boiling over a fire.

'Lift the lid of the pot and see,' said the hen wife.

Anne lifted the lid of the pot but saw nothing other than a broth bubbling away. The hen wife seemed annoyed, telling her, 'Go home and tell your mother to keep the larder door bolted.'

The queen was angry when she heard this, as she knew that the princess must have eaten something, but she said nothing. The next day she sent Anne back to the hen wife, but this time she went to the door with her, to make sure that she didn't have anything to eat on the way. As Anne walked down the road she met some people who were picking peas and they gave her some to eat. When she lifted the lid of the pot for a second time nothing happened.

'Tell your mother that the pot can't boil without the fire,' said the hen wife.

The queen was very angry this time, as she knew that the girl must have eaten something, so on the third morning she went with her all the way to the hen wife's cottage, just to make sure. This time when Anne was told to lift the lid of the pot she again saw the broth bubbling away but suddenly a sheep's head popped up to the surface and stared at her. Then Anne's beautiful head fell off and the sheep's head jumped onto her shoulders and took its place. The queen and the hen wife laughed at her, but she could do nothing but weep. When the queen took her back to the castle and Kate saw her they both cried on each other's shoulder. Then Kate carefully wrapped up Anne's head in bandages and led her out of the castle. They walked and walked a long way, searching for a cure for Anne's condition and to escape the evil queen.

After a while they came to another kingdom and headed towards the castle. Kate knocked on the door and said that she had travelled a very long way and that her sister was ill. Since they were both very tired and hungry she asked if they had any work that she could do in return for a bed and something to eat. Soon she was given a job in the kitchen washing pots and peeling vegetables. However, Kate noticed that the castle was not a happy place, everyone seemed sad and there was no music or laughter. She was told that the king's eldest son was gravely ill and near to death. He was growing weaker every day by some sort of sorcery, but no one was brave enough to sit with him all night to find out the cause of it. Kate said that she would sit with him that night if she was paid a peck of silver and the king was happy to agree to this.

That night Kate was sat by the fireside cracking nuts when the clock struck midnight. Suddenly the prince's eyes opened and he got up and dressed. Then he slipped down the back stairs, followed by Kate, and headed to the stable where he saddled his horse, called for his hound and rode away into the night. Kate jumped up behind him; the prince never even noticed that she was there. As they rode through the woods Kate plucked nuts from the trees and put them into the pocket of her apron. Eventually they reached a large, green hill and the prince called out, 'Open! Open, green hill, and let the young prince in with his horse and his hound.'

'And his lady behind him,' said Kate.

The green hill opened and they rode inside. There was a beautiful hall within the hill, brightly lit and richly furnished. The prince got off the horse and was surrounded by beautiful fairy ladies who led him away to dance while Kate hid behind the door and watched. They danced with him all night long and if he swooned on a sofa they would fan him and then raise him up to dance again. This was what was wrong with him; he was being danced to death by the fairies. When the cock crowed the prince mounted his horse and Kate jumped up behind him and they rode back to the castle where he went back to his bed. Kate sat once more by the fire, cracking nuts and eating them.

The next morning the king was delighted to find her there. She said that he had passed a peaceful night. She was offered a peck of gold to sit with him for another night and she willingly accepted. Again she sat with the prince and it all went the same that night as it had done on the first night. The prince rose, saddled his horse and rode to the green hill to dance with the fairy ladies all night long. This time Kate hid behind the door and saw a small fairy child playing with a wand. She overheard one of the fairies say to another, 'If only Kate knew that three strokes of that wand would make her sister as beautiful as ever.'

Kate rolled nuts towards the fairy child and he dropped the wand and chased after them. Kate took the wand, slipped it into her apron pocket and left with the prince when the cock crowed.

The following morning the king was delighted to see Kate still sitting with his son. He asked her what price she would take to stay a third night with him. Kate asked to marry him, and so it was agreed. Kate then rushed off to the room where her sister was and gave her three strokes on the head with the wand. The sheep's head tumbled off and her own beautiful head jumped onto her shoulders just like she was before.

That night went the same as the first two, with the prince riding to the green hill and dancing with the fairy ladies. Kate hid behind the door and saw the fairy child was playing with a brightly coloured bird. She overheard one of the fairies say to another, 'If only Kate knew that three bites of that bird would cure the sick prince.'

She rolled nuts over the floor towards the child who dropped the bird and ran after them. Kate grabbed the bird, put it in her apron pocket and left with the prince when the cock crowed.

That night, instead of sitting cracking nuts by the fireside, Kate plucked the bird and started to roast it over the fire. Soon a delicious aroma filled the room and the prince opened his eyes and said, 'Oh, if only I had a bite of that bird.'

Kate gave him a bite and the prince raised himself up on one elbow and said, 'Oh, if only I had another bite of that bird.'

Kate gave him a second bite and the prince sat up and said, 'Oh, if only I had a third bite of that bird.'

Kate gave him a third bite and the spell was broken. When the king came into the room the following morning he saw Kate and the prince sitting by the fire, cracking nuts together. He was delighted and the wedding was arranged. The prince had a brother and when he saw Anne, looking so beautiful again, he fell in love with her and they were married too. So the sick prince married the well sister and the well prince married the sick sister and they lived there in peace and happiness for the rest of their days and never drank out of a dry cup.

WESTERN ISLES

IAN STEPHEN

IAN STEPHEN was born and brought up on the Isle of Lewis, where he still lives. His mother's family were well-known storytellers, and his father's Scottish east coast background brought him to another strand of spoken culture.

A former coastguard officer, he has worked in the arts and pursued his passion for sailing since winning the inaugural Robert Louis Stevenson Award in 1995. He is the author of A Book of Death and Fish *and a selection of poems,* Maritime *(Saraband).* Waypoints: Seascapes and Stories of Scotland's West Coast *(Bloomsbury, 2017) was shortlisted for the Saltire Scottish non-fiction award.*

SOUTH UIST: ASKING FOR THE WIND

There was the storyteller and there was the bard. Some would say that the storyteller could take you through the range of human emotions while the bard could recite fluent and eloquent language to celebrate the family who was supporting him. But I don't think it could ever have been as simple as that. There are bards who wrote satire and those who celebrated ordinary people who could never pay the one who composed the verse. And there are storytellers who could make the language ring as fluently as any rhythmic verse.

But then there were the MacVurichs. People say that the output of this family of bards, who composed across the centuries, amounted to cartloads of manuscripts, but that all of it was of high quality. You can judge for yourselves because much of it has been kept safe. Some people say that poetry is powerful and others say that it changes nothing. There are many traditions to say that at least one MacVurich had astonishing powers. The family lived at Staligarry in South Uist and wrote countless lines to commemorate the doings of the Clanranald chiefs. But when times were lean in the bardic business, MacVurich would use his skills in navigation to ferry people back and fore from Skye. And they also said that his famous eloquence could have strange powers.

MacVurich had put in to Canna. They met a merchant who was keen to return to Arisaig, over on the mainland. MacVurich's son was also aboard and was very keen to get home. Maybe this lad was courting, back on the Uists. What do you do, as a skipper, when everyone aboard wants to go to a different place? And most skippers are content to get a mild, fair wind, without too much drama, though they'll deal with a gale if they meet it.

The skipper said that each should raise his voice to request the wind that would suit his purpose. But he used his rank and put in a very fair request for the warm south-westerly, which would put the wind a little behind their beam as they made to clear Usinish Point and tuck in to the safety of Loch Skiport. There's an anchorage in there, called the Wizard's Pool, where no wind will bother a vessel. This was his formula:

A south wind from calm Gailbhinn,
as the King of Elements ordained;
one we could ride without rowing or tacking,
a breeze that could bring us no harm.

MacVurich quoted from a goatherd of the King of Norway who felt he was in a warm, fertile and temperate land when he set foot on 'Gailbhinn', which could well be Galway. So that would be a temperate south-westerly breeze, taken mid-ships or, as he would have said, *ga ruith air a tarsainn*. Now they could cross where he wanted, on one tack.

'What kind of a soft skipper have we got here?' said the merchant. 'She could take a wind with a bit more body in it. And one that could take me at once to my next port of call.'

'Well you can ask for it yourself,' MacVurich said. Not for the first time, one action, not fatal in itself to safe navigation, set off a chain of events. This was the merchant's plea:

A North wind, hard as a rod of iron
to raise her gunwales high on the crests,

so she has the strength and speed of a hind
running down the hard peak of a hill.

Before long, there was indeed a backing of the wind, to
the tune of 180 degrees. The building waves threw her
bow off their course and they had no option but to run
before it, taking it on their port quarter. This was a fast
and exhilarating point of sail, a broad reach to take her,
nearly surfing, as her rounded, buoyant stern lifted on the
following seas (*Ga ruith air a sliasaid*). It looked like they
might be bound for Arisaig after all. But there was one
request still to be said. Mind you, they also say you should
never make use of that third one. It's a bit like unleashing
the last knot.

MacVurich, the skipper, had referred to the land
favoured by the King's goatherd, the one who became a
smith like no other. That was a man who could temper the
sword of Finn to endow it with power. But now the skipper's son wanted home and did his best to raise the wind
that would turn them round again. The lad referred to
one of the strongest of the Fingallian warriors. Even Finn
was relieved when Conan placed his spear with the Fianna
rather than against them. Now the son of MacVurich
looked to wake his spirit:

If in cold hell there's a wind
that turns the waves' sides to red,
Conan, send it after me
in fiery flaming sparks.

It wouldn't matter, he said, if the power of it was such that
only his father, himself and their black dog could take it.

That's what they got, all right. The boat was whipped round, beyond the control of anyone aboard it. It was driven by the squalls that came from clouds like anvils, looming from the heights above the jagged line of the Cuilins of Rum. There was hail and there was lightning. They had to let go the halyard and pull all cloth down. Now they were running (*ga ruith air a deireadh*) where the wind and waves drove them, pushed by the gale on the bare pole. She was driven into a place, close to Usinish Point. She came ashore with a crack that broke her in two. They were lucky to escape with their lives and even the dog had a struggle in reaching dry land. All of them were beyond caring what land they stood on, as long as it was solid ground.

'What a chasm you took us into,' MacVurich's son said, though it was his own verse that had done the damage.

'Well I don't think we'll try that again,' his father said. 'From now on, we'll just put up with the wind we get.'

But to this day, the place where they made their landfall is still called A Ghiamraidh or 'The Chasm'.

❖

References
This telling uses elements from several versions including recordings of Angus MacLellan and two from Martin MacIntryre, of Skye, made by D.A. MacDonald. Angus MacLellan's telling of this story is in *Stories From South Uist*, edited and translated by John Lorne Campbell. There is also a recording from 1963–64 of the same teller by D.A. MacDonald, held at the School of Scottish Studies, ref 42782 SA 1963.016. Several other versions of the

MacVurich traditions are held and can be heard on www. tobarandulchais.co.uk.

Stories From South Uist also contains transcriptions of Angus MacLellan's retelling of Fingallian legends and some of the details relating to the allusions to Gailbhinn and Conan are taken from there. For a full and fluent retelling of Irish legends, see Mary Heaney, *Over Nine Waves* (Faber and Faber, London, 1994).

For a full collection of Gaelic maritime terminology and traditions see George MacLeod (of Great Bernera), *Muir is Tìr: Seòras Chaluim Sheòrais* (Acair, Stornoway, 2005).

Wit is much prized, as well as eloquence, in the oral culture of the Western Isles. Mrs Mary Ann MacInnes of Stilligarry was recorded by D.A. MacDonald quoting the response of one of the MacVurichs to the offer of a very meagre bowl of milk from Dunvegan of Skye and published in the School of Scottish Studies journal *Tocher* no. 57. He saw a fly floating in it and addressed it, 'Poor thing, you should never have drowned. You didn't need to swim. You could have waded through that.' (Quote paraphrased here.)

LEWIS AND OUTLYING ISLANDS: WHO WAS CHASING WHO?

Every culture, rural or urban, has its bogeyman stories. On the Island of Lewis the figure was known as Mac an t-Sronaich. Sometimes this is translated as 'son of the long-nosed one', but most people seem to think there was a real live person, who hailed from the district of Sronaich, on the mainland. There is some evidence that there was a vagrant or nuisance but little evidence that this man really did commit murder. That did not stop my uncle Kenny Murdo Smith from telling tale after tale, which I now know came from his own father. As children, we loved to be scared when our uncle was babysitting.

The way I remember his stories, people, especially bright youngsters, quite often got the better of the outlaw. Every district seems to have its own cave linked to the fugitive. If he used every one of them, he got around even more than Bonnie Prince Charlie, who also has many points and cairns with his name on them.

In Stornoway they say that Mac an t-Sronaich was given some shelter and food at the window of a manse across the moor, in Keose. The minister's wife was related in some way.

Some stories are still surfacing and my favourite is very much in sympathy with the tone of those told me by my uncle.

❖

Mac an t-Sronaich ranged wide and far over the moors and took what he wanted to keep himself alive. It seems he reached as far as the district of Uig and further, over the hills till you were close to the remote communities at Tamnavay and at the head of Loch Resort. They say that two men set off to join the cliff path by Scarp, to buy a piggy of whisky for a *reitach* or a wedding. When they failed to return, it was found that they had paid their money and taken the jar but neither of them were seen again. Nor was the whisky.

That was the sort of deed folk said must have been the work of Mac an t-Sronaich, but I could think of a few other possible explanations for the disappearance of these men. Not so far from that terrain, another chase took place.

The herring would come in to Loch Tamnavay in season. It was thick with them and good hauls could be made. But one village lost their herring net to an army of dogfish that left it in tatters. At other times that would have been another blessing, for the oil from the liver of that species was valuable. But it was a curse when the herring were at their prime. They were full fish, at the height of the summer.

So one fit fisher-lad, by the name of Dohmnall Ruadh Beag, set off to cover the miles over the moor to bring back a replacement. It was heavy and sweaty work, with all these yards of treated cotton, in a parcel, draped around his shoulders.

The ties broke and he just gathered the whole dark thing, dangling corks and all, about his chest. He was barefoot of course, so he just rolled his breeks up to his thighs and enjoyed the relief of the cool damp peaty ground on his warm feet and ankles.

What he didn't know was that Mac an t-Sronaich was stalking him, looking to come in and steal what he could, when his man weakened. He drew in closer when Dohmnall Ruadh Beag was about to descend at *Beinn a Deas*. But when he crept over a mound he saw a strange creature, like a giant insect, with a dark web around its broad shoulders and white spindly legs under that.

He took to his heels at once. Mac an t-Sronaich was known to be a fierce wiry man who could fight anything human, but this had to be a creature from another terrible world. He thought the hardy wee redhead was the devil himself.

❖

References
Based on Maggie Smith's recording of Finlay MacIver: www.hebrideanconnections.com/Details.aspx?subjectid =8596. See also the same informant's description of curing haddock:

> It wasn't left in the salt for very long at all. They used to say that if you took the eyes out of the haddock, as much salt as the two hollows would hold, that that was enough to salt the fish. Too much salt and it was far too salty. Then they hung it above the fire. In the winter it was half smoked and it kept them in meals until the spring. It was soaked first of all to remove part of the salt.

THE HIGHLANDS

BOB PEGG

In a career lasting over half a century, musician, songwriter and storyteller BOB PEGG has performed in venues ranging from a Viking longhouse in the wilds of Iceland, to the Royal Festival Hall in London. He organised the Tales at Martinmas festival in Ross-shire, and was the director of the Merry Dancers Project, which brought storytelling to schools and communities the length and breadth of the county, from Cromarty to Applecross. He lives in Strathpeffer.

THE SEAL KILLER

Duncansby Head is a little to the north of John O'Groats. Some years ago, I walked from the lighthouse there, down towards the stacks that protrude from the seabed like giant prehistoric arrowheads. In the bay, the black heads of a dozen or so seals rose and turned to look up at me, reminding me of the many stories which tell of the people of the sea.

In a cottage on Duncansby Head, there was once a man who made his living from killing seals. When he had killed them he would strip off the skins to make trousers and waistcoats, boots that were called rivlins, and small purses for ladies to keep their money in.

Six days a week, he would climb down the steep path to the beach, push out his boat, row into the middle of the bay, and wait for the seals to come to him. With him he took a little silver whistle which he had from his father, who had it from his father before him; and so on, back through the generations. With the whistle came a tune, a seal-calling tune. When he played, the seals would gather round the boat to listen.

One day the seal killer was out in the bay, playing his silver whistle, when a huge seal broke the surface of the sea, just by the boat. The seal killer put down the whistle and picked up his bone-handled knife. He plunged it deep into the back of the seal, just behind the head, but the seal was so large and powerful that it dived down beneath the waves, taking the knife with it.

The seal killer was astonished and dismayed. The knife had been passed down to him with the whistle. It was old, and knew how to do its job. He used it to kill the seals, and to skin them, and without it he couldn't carry on with his trade. He rowed back to the shore, climbed up the path, and entered his cottage. He sat down at the kitchen table with his head in his hands, and wondered how he could ever get another knife.

All day the seal killer sat. Evening brought a storm, thunder and lightning. The seal killer drifted in and out of sleep; then, after midnight, someone knocked. He went to the door and opened it. A tall man stood at the threshold, a stranger, with a black cloak wrapped round him, and a wide-brimmed black hat pulled down over his eyes.

'Are you the seal killer?'

'Yes I am. What do you want with me?'

'I've a job for you. You must come with me now.'

There was a flash of lightning, and the seal killer caught a glimpse of a black stallion standing patiently at the cliff edge. The tall stranger climbed into the saddle and pulled the seal killer up behind him, and they rode off into the mouth of the night. They rode through the deepest, darkest valleys, across raging torrents, over the highest mountain peaks, through rain and hail and sleet and snow, until they came to a high cliff top.

The stranger dismounted. So did the seal killer. The stranger wrapped his arms around the seal killer, and took a deep breath. He put his lips to the seal killer's lips, then he blew the air out into the seal killer's lungs, and threw himself off the cliff with the seal killer still in his arms. The two of them fell like stooping hawks until they hit the surface of the sea, and sank down to the ocean's bed.

When they reached the sea floor there was a door. They went through the door and they were in a hall full of brown-eyed, pale-faced, weeping people. The stranger took the seal killer into a smaller room. In the room, on a bed, lay a beautiful woman. She was so pale and still that it was impossible to tell whether she was alive or whether she was dead. The seal killer saw that the handle of his knife was sticking out of her shoulder. Then the stranger spoke.

'This is our queen – the Queen of the Selkie people. Yesterday morning you stabbed her in the back, and now you are the only one who can save her. You must pull out the knife and kiss the wound.'

What could the seal killer do but obey? He leaned forward, pulled out the knife and kissed the wound, and the wound closed over as if by magic. The woman opened her eyes and looked into the eyes of the seal killer, but before either of them had time to speak the stranger said, 'Right, that's your job finished. Come with me.'

He took the seal killer by the arm and led him back through the room full of brown-eyed, weeping people, 'til they came to the sea door.

'Now,' said the stranger, 'before I let you go, promise me one thing.'

'What's that?'

'You will never, ever kill another seal.'

'No, I never will kill another seal.'

'Right,' said the stranger, 'take this, and whatever you do, don't open it until you get home.'

The stranger reached under his cloak and pulled out a bundle. He pressed the bundle into the seal killer's hands, opened the sea door, and pushed him out into the darkness. The seal killer rose and rose through the dark waters until he thought the lungs would burst out of his body. Then his head broke the surface of the sea.

It was dawn, and he was in the bay below the cliff where his cottage stood. He swam to the shore and dragged himself dripping up the cliff path. He opened the door of the cottage and threw the bundle down onto the kitchen table. The bundle split open, and the kitchen was filled with gold coins.

The seal killer never did kill another seal. He lived out his life in the little cottage above the bay. He never married and he never had children. But the people who live in that part of the world say that, whenever the moon was full, he went down to the beach and stood at the edge of the sea. Then he took out a silver whistle, and played a tune. After a while, a great seal pulled itself up out of the sea, onto the shingle. Then the seal took off its skin, and out stepped a beautiful woman. All night long, she and the seal killer danced together on the beach. Then, when the sun rose, the Queen of the Selkies slipped back into her skin, and flopped away into the waves.

A HIGHLAND ORIGIN MYTH

The single-track road out of Lochcarron threads through the hills for a short while before it reaches the Bealach, a road which follows an old drovers' route. The Bealach is the steepest inclined road in Britain, ascending above Loch Kishorn in a series of hairpin bends to the top of Sgùrr a'Chaorachain and a view across to the Isle of Skye and the Cuillin mountains. Down below is the village of Applecross, where St Maelrubha, an Irishman from Derry, founded a monastery in the late seventh century.

The story doesn't begin or end here, but most of the action takes place in Applecross.

A long time ago – and I mean a very long time ago – Norway was full of giants. This was a situation left over from the time of the Norse gods, when the giants had their own territory, which was called Utgard. Though they weren't the brightest of beings, they managed quite well there, seldom coming unstuck unless one of them strayed into Asgard, the realm of the gods themselves, or unless one of the gods – Odin or Loki, and particularly Thor – made a foray into Utgard. Thor, who some might call a belligerent, red-bearded bully, was never happier than when he was laying into the giants with his famous hammer, Mjölnir.

Snorri Sturluson's *Edda* says that after Ragnarök, the battle to end all battles, both gods and giants perished, but this isn't entirely true. Many of the giants, male and female, had been far too slow on the uptake to get to Ragnarök in time for the final conflict, and they were left wandering aimlessly in a wasteland, waiting for the beginning of the world as we know it today.

This is how, when civilisation did arrive, Norway came to be full of giants.

On the whole, giants and humans got on pretty well together. There was the occasional brawl – lady giants sometimes took a shine to gentleman humans – but disputes of that kind will arise in any close-knit community. Generally speaking, although a certain amount of mutual partying went on at the weekends, giants and humans tended to go home to their own beds and dream their respective dreams.

Just occasionally, though, a rogue giant would surface, and everything would be thrown off kilter. There was a giant called Thrim, a survivor from the bad old days, who hated humans. He lived high up in the mountains so, for a long time, he caused no trouble, but in time his hatred grew so intense that he began to make excursions down into the valley villages, rampaging around, biting off the heads of humans, sucking out their vital juices, and tossing away the skin and bone. As he advanced on an unsuspecting community or an isolated farmstead, Thrim would roar, 'I'm gonna find you! I'm gonna catch you! I'm gonna eat you!'

This behaviour was intolerable to both humans and giants, who had worked hard to live together in peace, so they convened a council and voted to expel Thrim from Norway.

Thrim wasn't greatly bothered by this decision. He was happy to follow his lust for human juice wherever it might lead him, so he headed out for the place we now call Scotland. The North Sea was much shallower then, and Thrim strode through waters which seldom rose above his knees, announcing as he went, 'I'm gonna find you! I'm gonna catch you! I'm gonna eat you!'

After a couple of days' wading, the giant reached Shetland. The islands were even more sparsely populated than they are today, and most of the inhabitants were trolls, or 'trows', more refugees from Ragnarök, who thought the universe had passed them by until Thrim came storming over the horizon. He didn't spend long in Shetland. In truth, the blood of the trows – green, viscous stuff – tasted so vile that even Thrim couldn't stomach it. He didn't bother to stop in Fair Isle – more trows – but there were enough humans on Orkney to detain him for a while. The few who escaped hopped into their boats and made for the mainland – for Caithness, as it's now called – leaving the islands as easy pickings for a Viking takeover a couple of millennia later. Once Orkney was devoid of humans, Thrim pursued the refugees across the Pentland Firth to Caithness. Splashing through the Swelkie whirlpool, he yelled at the distant mountains of Sutherland, 'I'm gonna find you! I'm gonna catch you! I'm gonna eat you!'

There's no precise record of the devastation that Thrim left in his wake on his progress across the Highlands. Occasionally archaeologists on a dig will come across an isolated skull which has no body nearby, and they will wonder about the strange rituals of our ancestors; and there are geological faults which can best be explained as resulting from the impact of giant footsteps. But all we know for sure is that eventually Thrim came to the west coast, to the Applecross peninsula in the region which is now called Wester Ross. The great mountain called Sgùrr a'Chaorachain – the big conical hill of the blaze or the torrent – comes between Applecross and the rest of the mainland. From the far side of Sgùrr a'Chaorachain, the people of Applecross heard the distant cry of the approaching giant, 'I'm gonna find you! I'm gonna catch you! I'm gonna eat you!' But they were prepared for his coming. For weeks, tales of the gargantuan bloodsucker had been brought in by refugees from other parts of the Highlands. The presence of these refugees had started to cause problems – overcrowding and food shortages – and some of the Applecross folk were all for putting them on makeshift rafts and sending them over the sea to Raasay and Skye; but the Community Council held an extraordinary meeting, and came up with a plan.

A broad, deep pit was dug in the place where the Applecross campsite is today. Several dozen pine trees were felled and set in the bottom of the pit, then sharpened into massive stakes. For the next part of the plan, half a dozen of the cheekiest Applecross children were sent up Sgùrr a'Chaorachain. The goading, threatening voice of Thrim grew closer until, at last, a boulder-sized spiky head appeared above the highest peak, and the giant hove into view. As soon as they saw him, the cheeky children began to throw out taunts. 'Dim-wit lardybum' was the least of them.

The children, pursued by the raging, stumbling giant, skipped down the brae, across the heather and over the burns, knowing every inch of the land. At the bottom of the mountain they scattered. The giant, propelled by his own momentum, sped on downwards. The people of Applecross had stretched a tripwire across the path just before the stake pit. Thrim never even saw the wire (for giants are short-sighted). When his ankles hit it, he flew up into the air and revolved several times, before landing on the stakes, in the pit. With the giant impaled, the Applecross folk swarmed down, and set to work with whatever sharp implements they possessed. Pen-knives, hacksaws, hatchets, chainsaws were all used to dismember Thrim's body. After they had cut him into the tiniest pieces, they retired to the Applecross Inn to celebrate their victory, and in the early hours they straggled home to their beds. Some time in the night – nobody can remember exactly when – the people of Applecross were woken by a distant, muted voice.

'I'm gonna find you,' it whispered. 'I'm gonna catch you,' it murmured. 'I'm gonna eat you,' it mused.

Next morning, at dawn, they were out of their houses and down to the pit. There was no doubt that the tiny pieces of Thrim-flesh were still alive. They were jiggling around, and muttering angrily to themselves, 'I'm gonna find you... I'm gonna catch you... I'm gonna eat you...' The Applecross folk gathered as much kindling and dried seaweed as they could. They threw them into the pit, and tossed burning brands after them, and once there was a good blaze they fed it with chunks of peat. They watched all day until the fire slowly dwindled, and by evening there was nothing left at the bottom of the pit but a layer of fine ash.

The inhabitants of Applecross looked at each other in relief and began to speak for the first time in many hours. They agreed that they had done well to rid the world of the giant and felt it was time to celebrate (again) with a drink and a party. As they turned away from the pit a faint breeze came in from the sea, and lifted tiny specks of ash into the air. Each piece of ash began to speak, and thousands of little voices chorused, 'We're gonna find you... we're gonna catch you... we're gonna eat you.'

The ash cloud drifted towards the Applecross people. They began to run, pursued by a voracious horde which was, indeed, intent on eating them. These were the very first Highland midges. Although they began life in Applecross, they quickly spread up and down the west coast, out to the islands, and have even set up colonies in other parts of Scotland. If, like many unsuspecting visitors before you, you're caught out by them on some beautiful evening in Torridon, Gairloch, or Durness, listen, as you run for cover, for those little voices keening joyously, 'We're gonna find you! We're gonna catch you! We're gonna eat you!'

ABERDEENSHIRE

GRACE BANKS & SHEENA BLACKHALL

GRACE BANKS is a storyteller, singer and outdoor-discovery practitioner who is passionate about sharing her love of nature and story. She provides activities or projects for schools and other groups to encourage wonder, creative expression and understanding of the surrounding environment. Grace has recently produced a CD and outdoor resource booklet. Please check out her website: silverhaar.com.

SHEENA BLACKHALL BSc (Hons, Psych), Dip.Ed, M.Litt (Distinction), is a Scots writer, illustrator, and traditional ballad singer/songwriter. She is also a registered storyteller. From 1998-2003 she was Creative Writing Fellow in Scots at Aberdeen University's Elphinstone Institute. To date she has published three Scots novellas, 'Minnie',' Loon', and 'the Quarry'. With Les Wheeler she co-edits The Elphinstone Kist, www.abdn.ac.uk/elphinstone/kist, a Doric website with feely downloadable resources designed for use across the North East community and its diaspora beyond.

THE GIANT WITH THE THREE GOLDEN HAIRS, OR, THE SEELY CAP

(GRACE BANKS)

Of all the tales that Stanley Robertson gave to me, this has always been my favourite. Here is my retelling of it. – G.B.

When Jack was born into the safety of his mother's loving arms, he had no idea of the adventures that lay before him. His weary parents only hoped there would be enough food to fill yet another mouth, for Jack was the twelfth son of a twelfth son, born to a poor woodcutter and his wife.

Unlike the other bairns, this child was born with a seely cap that covered his head. The skin was removed by the midwife and placed reverently into the mother's hands. 'Dinna lose this seely cap,' she said, 'for yer son is born lucky, an' this is a charm that will keep ill awa' fae him.'

Ruling over the land was a cruel and merciless king. Word came to his ear of the child that had been born with good fortune smiling on him. In fact, it was said that the wise woman, the speywife, on seeing the bairn, had pronounced that he would one day marry the king's daughter and sit on his throne. Outraged, the king decided he would go to see this child for himself.

Making his excuses to his courtiers, the king left his castle behind him, and dressed as a rich merchant with cart and horse, he arrived at the forest where the poor family dwelt. He was taken into the crowded home and fed by a tired, thin woman. As he ate of the simple fare, his eyes darted around the room and alighted upon a well-worn cradle in the corner.

'Ye've a lot o' bairns?'

'Aye,' said the mother, with a gentle smile, 'anither een newly born tae!'

'May I see?' asked the man. She nodded, and brought over a warmly-wrapped and sleeping bundle. Her eyes shining, she said, 'This is our youngest son.'

The king made appropriate murmurs of appreciation.

'Another child tae tak care o'. That must be a thocht.' He caught the fleeting shadow of worry that crossed the mother's face and spoke again, silkily. 'You know, I hivnae bairns of ma' own. I wid gladly tak this small lad an' raise him.' The look of horror that crossed the mother's face only made the king more determined.

By the time the woodcutter had reached home, the king had almost persuaded the mother. The two parents anxiously spoke together, but agreed it would be in their son's best interests to be raised by the merchant.

The king left a heartbroken family with a satisfied smile on his face, and in the cart, the crude wooden cradle with a baby snuggled down within, his seely cap hidden beside him.

It was not long before the king found what he was looking for, a deep ravine through which rushed a roaring river. Without a second thought, the cruel man heaved the cradle and its contents over the cliff, and watched as it smashed into the river and disappeared below the surface.

Well pleased with his day's work, the king set off for home. But, had he stayed, he would have seen the cradle re-emerge at the surface, buoyed like a cork, and the child and seely cap, although soaking wet, driven downstream in their makeshift vessel.

Some hours later, a miller was woken by the sound of screaming. Rising, the man made his way down to the millstream. There, swirling in the shallows, was a cradle, and from within came the indignant screams of a wet and hungry bairn. The miller and his wife were a childless couple, and happily welcomed the river child into their home, bringing him up as their very own.

Years later, the king was out hunting, and after a long day, tired and thirsty, he came upon a mill where he was welcomed in and given refreshment by the wife and her handsome son.

'That's a fine boy ye hiv there, madam!' the king said, smiling his thanks as the lad refilled his cup of ale.

'Thank ye, sire,' said the mother, smiling proudly. 'This is Jack, oor lad fae the river.' 'Fit d'ye mean?' asked the king.

'Well, many years ago, a cradle was swept downstream, and we found Jack lying inside! We brought him up as our own!' The king managed to look interested and hide the anger and dismay that seethed in his breast. He looked at Jack and felt hate fill his heart, but his words were warm and friendly.

'Jack, yer a fine lookin lad. How wid ye like tae come an' work for me? Perhaps ye could be a sodger or work in ma palace?'

The king could be very persuasive, and by the time the miller had come home, it was all but decided that Jack would enter the king's service.

'Jack, can ye write?'

'No, sire,' the lad said, his cheeks reddening.

'Dinna worry, son,' the king said genially, 'I'm goin' tae be hunting for a few mair days, so I'll write a letter tae ma queen which ye must tak straight tae her when ye arrive.'

'Yes, yer Majesty,' said Jack, overcome by the sudden change in circumstances and not sure how he felt about them.

Amidst much sadness and promises to return, Jack set off the next day with a satchel of food, the sealed scroll for the queen and his seely cap placed carefully in his jacket pocket. The lad had been given directions, and by nightfall, he guessed he was about halfway to the palace. Rain was falling heavily, and seeing a light from a house, he approached the door and knocked. It was opened cautiously, and a frightened woman squinted out into the darkness.

'Good evenin'. May I come in?'

'No!' she cried, and slammed the door in Jack's face. The rain was driving down, and Jack was soaked, so he knocked again, this time more insistently. Again the door opened.

'Please!' he said, 'I'm soakin'! Jist a warm by yer fire, that's a' I ask!'

The woman looked at the lad, his fair hair plastered to his pale pleading face, and relented. 'On yer ain head be it then!'

She pulled the door wide for him to enter. With great relief, Jack felt the warmth of the fire beckoning, and soon his wet clothes were off and he was wrapped in a rough homespun blanket with the woman clucking over him and plying him with hot soup. Snug, warm and full, Jack lay down on the stone hearth and immediately fell asleep.

Later, the door opened again, and a troop of men entered, all weary, soaked and in a foul mood. They were robbers, and had suffered a bad day. When they saw Jack at the fireside, their first thought was to kill him, but the woman pleaded with them and showed what she had found in Jack's pocket.

'Weel, weel,' said the leader quietly, 'I've nivver seen a seely cap afore! Lads, we must treat this lad wi' respect, an look efter him!'

'An' see fit else wis in his pocket!' said the woman, passing over the sealed scroll to the man. All weariness forgotten, the thief sat down at the table and rubbed his damp hands dry. Then carefully, he unpicked the seal and opened the scroll. He read:

My dear,
When this vagabond hands you this scroll – listen tae this, lads – *please have him executed forthwith.*
Your loving husband,
King John.

The robber whistled. 'This lad has made an enemy o' the king! And we all are, are we not, lads?'

'Aye!' the men answered, grinning.

When Jack awoke the next morning, the woman was stoking the fire and there was breakfast laid out for him on the table. His clothes had been dried and neatly folded, and he checked the pockets to make sure the letter and his seely cap were still in place. After a good meal, he thanked the woman, who smiled at him fondly, and on he went.

He arrived at the palace, and on producing the scroll with the king's seal, he was taken directly to the queen's chambers.

He bowed low and presented the letter to her majesty.

A little confused, the queen opened the scroll, and this is what she read:

My dear,
When this fine lad hands you this scroll, please have him married to our daughter forthwith. He has proved himself to be true and worthy of her love.

Your loving husband,
King John.

The queen was not one to disobey her husband, and immediately set about arranging the wedding, which took place the following morning. For Jack and the princess, their marriage was not a burdensome demand, for one look had been enough to know how they felt about each other.

The king arrived home the following day to find himself in the midst of great joy and feasting. On questioning his wife, his face took on a look that chilled the queen's heart, and she knew fear. But as a cloud passes from the sun, the king as quickly recovered, and gallantly welcomed his new son-in-law, despite noting with disgust the look of love between Jack and his daughter.

Later in the evening, when much wine had been drunk and everyone was mellow, the king said mildly, 'Ye ken, Jack, as ma' son-in-law, it wid hiv been customary for ye tae achieve some great feat tae win ma daughter's hand. Wid ye be willing tae please me by doin' this?' Jack did not notice the anxious look that passed between his wife and mother-in-law. 'Of course, sire, anythin' for you!'

'Good, Jack. In that case, I wid like ye tae find the giant wi' the three gowden hairs, an bring those hairs tae me!'

'Where dae I find this giant, sire?'

'Ower hill an moor, through glen an forest, until ye reach the great loch. On an island in that loch is where the giant lives.'

'Very well, yer Majesty,' said Jack, uncertain of his capabilities, 'I will leave at first licht.'

There was a sad parting between the newlyweds as Jack, uncomfortable on horseback, set out on his next adventure.

He travelled far, and by evening came to a village where he found hospitality for the night. However, he was struck by how dour the villagers were, and enquired as to why.

'Och!' said one man, 'this village wis renowned fer its wine! Wine that flowed reid an' rich fae that fountain in the village square. But noo it's dried up, an' we dinna ken why, an' noo we've nae wine an' abody's miserable!'

'Weel,' said Jack stoutly, 'I am journeyin' far tae the giant wi' the three gowden hairs, an' it is said he kens mony things hidden frae man. If I can, I will find oot an' come back an' tell ye!'

The next day he travelled on, and by nightfall arrived at another village, and saw how sad the villagers were here too. One woman told him, 'Fer years we've hid a wonderful aipple tree, an in season it bore gowden fruit, enough tae bring riches an' happiness tae each an' everyone. But these last twa years there's been nae fruit, an' we dinna ken why.'

'Weel,' said Jack, 'I'm awa' tae see the giant wi' the three gowden hairs, and if I can, I'll ask the reason for this an come back an' tell ye.'

Some days later, Jack saw he was nearing a huge silver loch. Far out over the water, he could see an island. There was a small ferryboat waiting at the shore, and in it a disagreeable-looking man, surrounded by a huge accumulation of wealth – coins, gold cups and jewels.

'Good day, sir,' said Jack politely, 'can ye please row me tae the island?'

'Get in, then! An' that'll be ain coin!' said the man grumpily.

Jack paid his fare, stepped into the boat and sat down, looking around at all the riches piled around him. 'May I ask ye a question, sir?'

The ferryman looked up at Jack from beneath his dark and furrowed brow. 'Aye.'

'Why, when ye hiv all this wealth, are ye still a ferryman?'

The man let out a huge sigh. 'Aye, if ye could tell me hoo tae leave this life, lad, I wid gladly gie ye a' these riches. This is an enchanted boat, an' I am trapped rowin' it, for I dinna ken hoo tae brak the spell!'

'Dearie me,' said Jack, shaking his head. 'Weel, I'm awa' tae see the giant wi' the three gowden hairs, an' if I can, I'll find oot an' tell ye on ma return.'

'If ye return,' said the man moodily. 'Mony dae not, ye ken!'

Jack was silent for the rest of the journey, wondering what fate awaited him.

From the shore, it did not take Jack long to reach the giant's huge, dark castle. When he rapped on the heavy oak door, the sound echoed cavernously within. The door opened slowly, and there, to his surprise, was a small woman.

'Oh!' said Jack, 'good day!'

'Fit are ye doin here, lad?' said the woman worriedly.

'The king has sent me tae get three gowden hairs frae the giant who bides here.'

The woman looked horrified. 'The king sent ye tae yer death, ye mean!' Then, with surprising strength, she grabbed Jack's coat and hauled him in through the door.

'Hiv ye any idea o' the danger yer in, laddie?' she barked as she dragged Jack through to the kitchen.

'I'm beginning to …' he said meekly. At the fear in his voice, the woman looked at him, and her angry expression softened. 'Yer jist a bairn, look at ye!'

With that, she sat him down, and Jack told her his story, of his seely cap and his journey, marrying the king's daughter, and how he had come to be at the giant's castle. When he had finished, the woman looked at Jack. 'Well, I think I'll jist hiv tae help ye, lad. Noo the giant will be returnin soon, an' ye must hide, or else he'll hae ye fer supper!'

It was a few minutes later that there was a huge wrenching of the door and a voice roared, 'WUMMAN! FAR'S MA SUPPER?'

Thundering footsteps deafened Jack as the giant trudged through to the kitchen. The woman rushed around, speaking soothingly to the huge ogre. Jack could hear sounds of food being placed before the giant, and then slurps and crunchings as he ploughed his way through six oxen.

Replete at last, the giant belched an almighty belch. 'Now, wumman, croon me tae sleep!' The giant lay down on the ground, his huge ugly head heavy in the little woman's lap. At once, she began singing softly, and very quickly, Jack could hear the sound of snoring … then, 'OWWW! FIT DID YE DEE THAT FORRR?' The woman had pulled out one of the giant's golden hairs!

'Oh, sorry, ma' dear, it wis a fly. I thocht it wid wak ye, so I tried tae slap it awa',' she said, as she stuffed the golden hair into her apron pocket. 'Noo yer a wee bit wakened, could ye tell me somethin that's bin puzzlin me?'

'Fit?' asked the giant gruffly.

'The village that his a wine fountain, fit why does the wine nae langer flow?'

'There's a toad underneath the fountain. If they dig it oot, the wine will flow again … noo let me … sleep …'

Soon snores could be heard again, followed by another huge yelp from the giant. 'WUMMAN!' he roared, 'FIT ARE YE DEEIN!?'

'Oh, I'm so sorry, ma' dear. It wis a spider that time!' She placed the second golden hair in her pocket. 'But as yer wakened, can ye please tell me why the villagers wi' the gowden aipple tree nae langer hae ony fruit?'

'There's a rat gnawin at the roots! If they remove it, the tree will bear fruit again … noo … let me sleep …'

For the third time, the sound of snoring filled the kitchen, only to be followed by an earth-quaking screech! 'AGAIN!!?'

'Oh, ma' dear, that wis a nasty ant that time. It wis jist awa' tae bite ye!' She tucked the third hair away. 'But as yer wakened, ye ken the ferryman?'

'AYE!'

'How can he leave his boat?'

'A' he must dee is haund ower the oars tae anither, an' he will be free … noo, YE MAUN LET ME SLEEP!' The woman hurriedly began to stroke the ogre's face once more, singing softly until his loud snores drowned out her voice.

Very carefully, she took the three golden hairs from her pocket and handed them to Jack, who had slipped out from his hiding place. With a mouthed 'thank you' and a grin, he turned and made his way quietly from the castle.

When Jack reached the ferryman, the man looked up at him in amazement, and hope was in his eyes. 'Ye made it, lad! Well? Did he tell ye the answer?'

'Tak me tae the far shore an' I promise tae tell ye,' said Jack.

When he hopped out of the boat onto the sand, Jack turned to the man. 'The next man that seeks the ferry, gie him the oars, an' the enchantment will be broken, an' you will be free tae gang far ye please!'

The ferryman's eyes filled with tears of gratitude. 'Och, lad, I dinna ken hoo tae thank ye, but noo ye maun tak a' these riches. I'm sick tae the death o' them!'

When Jack arrived back at the castle, he was leading his horse, for he had bought a cart to contain all the riches he had been given. Not only had the ferryman insisted on giving him all he had, but the villagers whose apple tree now flourished had gratefully laden him with golden fruit. From the other village, he had been gifted with many bottles of the richest red wine. The princess, the queen, and the courtiers at the palace were overjoyed to see Jack return, but the king was not.

Jack presented his father-in-law with the three hairs, but he was not interested in them, and cast them aside. Instead he looked with jealousy on the riches Jack now possessed.

'Where did you take all this from?' he growled.

'These treasures were given tae me, yer Majesty, an' thanks tae you and the giant wi' the gowden hairs, I hiv made mony freens on the road!'

The next day, the queen discovered that the king had gone. He had decided to journey to seek riches for himself, with help from the giant on the island. His envy of Jack gnawed at him, and his greed for possessions consumed him.

He passed through the villages where Jack had been so welcomed, but his bitter gaze was seeking riches, and he found none in the smiles and kindness people showed.

When the king eventually reached the great loch, he found the ferryman waiting in his empty boat, a smile on his face. Approaching, he snarled, 'You there, I am yer king. Ye'll row me over to the island richt noo!'

'Yes, yer Majesty, of course,' said the ferryman merrily. 'If ye can jist hop into the boat an' hold the oars fer jist a wee moment …'

At the palace, the queen, the princess and Jack waited in vain for the king to return. When it appeared that he had gone for good, there was no great mourning in the castle, but rather the joyful coronation of a new king and queen.

The couple had wonderful children of their own, and Jack's parents were brought to stay at the palace. And so it was that Jack and his queen lived contented, and ruled wisely for the rest of their days.

FRENCH KATE

(SHEENA BLACKHALL)

From 1925 to 1965 my aunt, Mrs Helen Strachan, ran her bus service from Aberdeen to Braemar, along both the North and South Deeside roads. It ferried coffins, livestock, climbers, hikers, and tourists. During the war, a party of Canadian lumberjacks squeezed into the boot of the bus, to share the space with a crate of bantams and two old bikes, to get to a local dance through a blizzard. My father, Charles Middleton, was her manager, and her daughters, brothers, sisters and nephews etc. were variously employed as clippies and drivers. When the business ended, Pipe Major Norman Meldrum of Invercauld led a procession of forty buses and 200 people out of Braemar to close a chapter of Deeside's history. A main part of the summer trade was composed of day trips up nearby glens, with the driver telling passengers the local legends. A big hit was always the story of French Kate. – S.B.

> Bonnie lassie, will ye go, will ye go, will ye go
> Bonnie lassie, will ye go to the birks o' Abergeldie?
> Ye shall get a gown o' silk, a gown o' silk a gown o' silk
> Ye shall get a gown o' silk an a coat o' calliemankie.

Craig nam Ban, or the hill of the woman, near Abergeldie, is covered with magnificent birch and oak woods, and has in its side a cave where once a Pictish chief hid when his men were defeated and his tribe was scattered. The castle of Abergeldie sits on the south side of the Dee, and is rich with bartizans, sculptures and turrets, alongside a clock with a bell striking the hour. It is a sixteenth-century tower house, built by the Gordons in 1550. Birch wine was once brewed here in abundance, as well as whisky, in the many illicit stills around the area.

When King George VI and his brother Bertie (King Edward VIII) stayed in the castle, they thought that the tower, infested by bats, was haunted by the ghost of a young witch burned to death locally. It is a fact that the commissioners appointed for the trial of witches on 6 April 1597 ordered that the Laird of Abergeldie be 'charged for the compearance before them at Aberdeen of Janet Guissett, accused of witchcraft'. However, this is not the witch that haunts the tower, but rather the young, ill-fated *Caitir Fhrangach* or French Kate, otherwise known as Kitty Rankine, a young French girl who acted as maid to the Lady Gordon. There are Rankines to this day living on Deeside, so the name lived on after the girl's death.

The tale is an old one, easily told. The lord of the castle was away in France on business, and his lady was lonely and jealous. As women have done since time immemorial, she turned to the Black Arts to see if she could divine whether or not her husband was remaining faithful to her on his long journey away from home. Kitty Rankine, her maid, was a noted practitioner of the soothsayer's skills. The lady decided to avail herself of Kitty's abilities.

The girl was taken before her mistress, and told to use her power to reveal how the lord of the castle was spending his time. She peered into a magic mirror, obscured by mist. At a word from her, the mist cleared, and the Lady Gordon could clearly see her husband wooing a young and attractive French woman on his way home from France.

'Is this how my lord treats me? You have the means to strike him down. Drown the wretch!' cried the lady.

And so, Kitty Rankine had a huge cauldron taken to the top of the castle to be filled with water, and an empty wooden bowl set floating on it, like a gallant ship on the sea. Down went the young witch, down to the castle cellar, and there she began to incant a spell for raising a storm. Kitty could control wind, rain, thunder and lightning using the magic she had learned. First, she dug a hole in the earth of the cellar, poured a little water in it, and cutting a strand of her long fair hair, stirred it into the mud, widdershins.

Round and round the wind I mix
Shake a boat with eildritch tricks
Bring a storm to all on board
Let it founder, ship and lord.

Away up in the tower, the water in the cauldron began to shiver. Waves appeared on the surface and the wooden bowl began to rock unsteadily. As Kitty's chanting grew louder, the waves in the bowl grew higher and higher. Soon, the wooden bowl was being flung about like seeds in a sieve.

All this time, the Lady Gordon looked on, tight-lipped. The water leaped up and down wildly in the cauldron, spilling and splashing over the sides. Then the wooden bowl was swamped by a large wave, and sank.

'As in the cauldron, so at sea,' Kitty told her mistress. 'Your husband's drowned, along with his fancy woman.'

The lady began to hope that Kitty Rankine's powers were not so strong. Perhaps her husband was safe after all. But then word came to the castle that the Lord of Abergeldie had been drowned in a terrible storm, which had whipped up from nowhere. None survived.

Now that the Lady of Abergeldie was a widow, she grew anxious that folk in the area would lay blame at her door. She condemned Kitty Rankine as a witch, and claimed the girl had acted out of malice against the family. Robert McKeiry, the wizard, was set on her trail. Immediately, she changed herself into a hare:

I shall go into a hare,
With sorrow and sych and meickle care.
And I shall go in the Devil's name,
Ay while I come home again.

But Robert McKeiry changed himself into a hound, until she cried out:

Hare, hare, God send thee care.
I am in a hare's likeness now,
But I shall be in a woman's likeness even now.

And from a hare to a woman, she changed herself into a mouse. But Robert McKeiry changed himself into a weasel and caught her by the tail. Wriggle as she might, he was more powerful than her, and she was forced to change into her human form.

They led her before the sheriff, and the verdict of guilty was swift. Caitir Fhrangach was taken, trussed like a roast, to the summit of Craig nam Ban, and there she was burned at the stake. To this day, men claim to hear her ghostly death screams echoing over the dark waters of the Dee.

PERTHSHIRE

LINDSEY GIBB & C.A. HOPE

LINDSEY GIBB loves stories and has been telling and sharing them all her life. Her connection to the land and all that dwells on it comes through in her storytelling. She is a member of the Directory of Storytellers in Scotland, and has been performing and leading workshops throughout Scotland and further afield for many years.

C.A. HOPE lives and works in Perthshire, usually writing biographical novels, but found the change of genre fascinating. C.A. firmly believes in keeping folk tales alive, as they are a vital connection to a very important aspect of our past.

LINDSEY and C.A. became friends when working in wildlife conservation, and were delighted when the opportunity arose to write Perthshire Folk Tales together. They believe Jaffa Cakes are an important food group.

THE GOLDEN CRADLE OF THE PICTS

Over a thousand years ago the great country we now call Scotland was in the grip of power struggles between the Vikings, the Scots and the Picts. Stories handed down through generations provide a vivid picture of relentless violence. Bloody battles raged, driven by both intelligence and brawn, and the wily strategies to take control of the people and land became the stuff of legend.

One such tale has lasted the test of time and concerns the town of Abernethy in the middle years of the ninth century.

At dawn on a summer morning, King Drust of the Picts set out from his stronghold at the base of Castle Law with the last of his warriors. Years of fighting had reduced them to a motley force but they marched proudly behind their King, standards waving, their loved ones cheering and crying until they were out of sight.

King Drust knew his reign was coming to an end. He was heading north to Scone to face Kenneth Alpin (Cináed mac Ailpín), King of the Scots. There are two versions of the terrible events which occurred that day, and which one you believed depended on whether you were a Pict or a Scot.

Some say the Scots set a deadly trap for King Drust. The two enemies were meeting for an uneasy banquet at Scone where there was much revelry, music and dancing, with Kenneth's serving girls keeping the goblets well-filled with liquor. While the Picts were in a jovial, numbed state, the Scots made their move. Pulling out pegs from under the long trestle seats, they dropped their enemies into prepared trenches filled with blades and sharpened spikes.

The other version tells us King Drust led the charge against the King of the Scots on the battlefield and was cut down and killed amid the bluster and courage of the fight.

Either way, King Drust was killed.

Fleet-footed runners rushed south over hills and through glens to carry the tragic news back to the Pict's fort at Abernethy. Before leaving, King Drust had warned his wife and all the members of his household of the inevitable Scots' victory, so the news was not unexpected. They recalled his passionate words, urging them to make the best of their lives under the Scots rather than be needlessly slaughtered before their time.

Nevertheless, on hearing confirmation of his death, the fort erupted into wailing, cursing, arguing chaos. It would not be long before Kenneth's soldiers would be at the door to take their gold and quash any revival. The older folk believed they should stand firm: they were Picts until the day they died and would not submit to the Scots. Others felt it was futile and started to unbar the door, preparing to kneel before their victors and keep their heads on their shoulders.

Up in one of the attic rooms, King Drust's faithful old nursemaid scoured the horizon for any sight of approaching Scots. She was disgusted by the feeble cries of defeat and had a far more important subject on her mind. While the queen wept and wrung her hands downstairs in the main hall, the old nurse moved rapidly to take action.

Ever since he was born, when she cared for him as an infant, King Drust had trusted her implicitly. In recent years, he had made her responsible for the two most valuable things in his life and she knew these two things would be the first to be taken by the King of the Scots: his baby son and the cradle in which he lay.

The golden cradle was an ancient royal heirloom. Wrought from solid gold, nobody knew where it came from nor who created such a wondrous work of art, only that every baby born to a Pictish king was laid in this cradle. Oh, how much the King of the Scots would want to own this potent symbol of the Picts!

She knew what she must do. She knew she couldn't pick up the cradle. It was very, very, heavy and had remained as if stuck to the floor for many a year. There was no time to lose but she could barely even drag it across the floorboards so she ran down to the kitchens. Within minutes she was back in the attic with the baby's devoted young nursery maid and a brawny but brainless young man. They clustered around the golden cradle and managed to haul it down the back stairs, baby and all. Leaving the fort by a secret door, they scurried towards the cover of trees overhanging a burn and headed up Castle Law, staggering and slipping beneath their burden. Behind them came the terrifying sound of the approaching spear-wielding Scots, King Kenneth riding at the front.

The nursemaid may have been in advancing years but her heart and lungs were strong. All the way up Castle Law she muttered under her breath. Bullying and encouraging the servants to keep going, she vowed to stop the cradle and the infant king from falling into the Scots' hands.

When they reached a shoulder on the hill they paused for breath, looking down at the besieged fort. Below them, one of the Scots' soldiers noticed the sunshine glinting off the radiant gold and a cry went up! Kenneth's sharp eye recognised the cradle and he set off in pursuit with a group of soldiers.

By the time they came over the brow of the hill, the nursemaid had moved on towards a loch. It was here, at the lochside, that they found her: alone.

She was sitting waiting for them on a rock above the water. The ribbons on her cap neatly tied, her skirts arranged over her knees, bare feet dangling in mid-air and her arms locked around the golden cradle. It seemed to the watching Scots that she took a breath, or perhaps she was speaking, for her mouth gaped open and her eyes focused on them as she pitched forward and plunged into the water.

King Kenneth shouted urgently to his men to dive in and retrieve the precious golden cradle, adding as an afterthought for them to save the royal baby. Shields and armour were unstrapped, heavy boots hastily unlaced with shaking, exhausted fingers but in these few short moments the hot summer day grew dark. Black clouds appeared, swirling overhead to send raindrops pelting down, whipping the loch's surface into a white froth.

Up from the water rose a colossal wave, its crest falling in an endless waterfall to rise again and again, twisting into the shape of a bony, writhing old crone. Her watery cloak billowed out from around her shoulders and the raging gale swept back her straggling white hair to show jagged features and oversized, staring eyes. Deep, resonating sounds reverberated through the ground like thunder, but it wasn't thunder. Words spilled from the towering supernatural creature in a voice so low and so loud and so shocking they were hard to decipher; even King Kenneth dropped to his knees.

Her warning given, the old hag disappeared back into the depths, leaving the rain hammering down through an eerie silence. Terrified and defeated in their quest for the golden cradle, King Kenneth and his men made their way off the hill, not daring to look back.

And what of the heir to the Pict throne, King Drust's baby son? Did that fiercely loyal nursemaid really drown her little charge, as she wished King Kenneth to believe? Or, did she sacrifice herself to divert attention from the little maid slipping away over the hills with a baby in her arms? If so, the bloodline of our ancient Pictish kings is still alive: somewhere.

Tantalisingly, a long time ago, golden keys were found in a local stream:

On the Dryburn Well, beneath a stane
You'll find the key o' Cairnavain
That will mak a' Scotland rich, ane by ane.

These keys are said to release the hoard of Pictish gold which was hastily and secretly buried between Castle Law and Cairnsvain on that fateful day.

The words spoken to King Kenneth and his soldiers by the old hag from the water gave clues of how to claim the cradle from the loch. The exact words have been lost from memory but are loosely recalled as meaning a man (or woman) should go alone to the lochan at dead of night. They must go round the loch nine times, encircling it with green lines and only then will they find the golden cradle.

For anyone thinking of trying to retrieve the golden cradle, a caution should be given. Although many have attempted this feat, none have succeeded and, more worryingly, many have either lost their wits or never been seen again.

THE URISK OF MONESS BURN

Before the noise and bustle of the Industrial Age drove them from the land, water sprites lived in almost every waterfall in Breadalbane. Tales of these faerie folk show some people describing them as goblins while others saw them as wee people with long flowing hair and often wearing bonnets.

Urisks were keen on food, very keen on food! They had a great love of fish and, in particular, milk. This may be why they made themselves useful to mortals by carrying out tasks like threshing their corn or other necessary jobs to be repaid in milk.

You would be mistaken, however, to assume urisks were always benign, good-humoured creatures. They were also well known for their naughty and downright destructive nature if they were upset. Unfortunately, being unpredictable was another aspect to their character, which sometimes made it hard to live with them as close neighbours.

This tale concerns the urisk they called Peallaidh (the Shaggy One). His full name was Peallaidh an Spuit and he lived among the rocks and waters of the Upper Fall of the Moness Burn, above Aberfeldy. His friend, a fellow urisk called Brunaidh an Easain (Broonie of the Smaller Fall), lived downstream on the lower waterfall.

Now, urisks are known for their longevity and it is claimed Aberfeldy was created by Peallaidh, the original Gaelic name being Obair Pheallaidh – The Work of Peallaidh.

Near Peallaidh's waterfall lived a farmer and his wife. Her turf-roofed cottage was always spick and span, her family well cared for and most days saw her humming away, preparing food over a glowing fire.

She was baking one day when Peallaidh came running in through her open door and snatched up her first batch of cooling bannocks.

The poor housewife was shocked and a little worried. If an urisk came into your home once, it would keep coming back. Out of the corner of her eye she watched the shaggy-haired little figure sitting at her table munching away at her scones. When the ones on the fire were ready, she tipped them on to the plate and hoped he would soon be full.

But no. As soon as Peallaidh's mouth was empty, with a savouring swallow and smack of his lips, he launched into one of the new ones. The woman stirred up more dough, deciding the only way to get rid of him was to fill this cheeky sprite until he could eat no more.

The woman's larder proved no match for the urisk's appetite. Soon, she feared he was going to eat all her food, leaving nothing for her family when they returned. She took longer than usual with the last batch, keeking over her shoulder from time to time to see when the urisk had finished the bannocks on the table.

'Here ye are,' she said pleasantly, using a cloth to pick up a new one, fresh from over the fire. She placed it straight into his hand.

With a screech of pain, Peallaidh dashed out the door. Shaking and blowing on his fingers, he fled through the ferns and birch trees to plunge his scalded fingers in the cold waters of Moness Burn.

At first, the woman was pleased to see him go and congratulated herself on getting rid of him. However, it was not long before she began chiding herself for hurting this affable wee sprite.

Up in his damp, dripping, trickling home under the torrents of the falls, Peallaidh was also mulling over his behaviour in a neighbour's home. Perhaps he had been a bit greedy? But the bannocks were delicious … then again, had he not seen her use the very last of her flour? Would her family go hungry that night? He was not proud of himself.

The next day, the farmer's wife soothed her conscience by placing a cup of milk and a bannock by the waterfall. When she returned the following day, the cup was empty and the bannock gone. A lifelong pattern emerged when every once in a while she repeated this gift.

Peallaidh did not come to her kitchen again. However, soon after, a large dry patch on her husband's field became unexpectedly moist and fertile. On searching for the source of the new spring, they followed it back to the upper waterfall.

The farmer's wife was not the only one making amends.

ARGYLL

BOB PEGG

In a career lasting over half a century, musician, songwriter and storyteller BOB PEGG has performed in venues ranging from a Viking longhouse in the wilds of Iceland, to the Royal Festival Hall in London. He organised the Tales at Martinmas festival in Ross-shire, and was the director of the Merry Dancers Project, which brought storytelling to schools and communities the length and breadth of the county, from Cromarty to Applecross. He lives in Strathpeffer.

THE SONG OF THE WIND

The grouping of stars in the tale The Magic Monster Bear *is the constellation we call the Plough, which itself is part of the larger constellation, the Great Bear.*

This happened long before the farming people put up the big stones and built the cairn tombs in Kilmartin Glen – and long before anyone had called the place by that name. In those days the land that wasn't saturated with water was covered over with forest. The first people came along the coast in boats made from wicker frames covered in hide. They made shelters in the caves at the edge of the sea, and they fished, ate the plants and berries that flourished in the forests, and hunted the animals which had drifted in as the ice sheet shrank northwards. At first they travelled around, never staying in one place for very long, following the bounties of fish, flesh and plant life that the successive seasons brought; but after a while they began to use axes with sharp flint heads to cut down the forest trees – oak, pine and hazel – and to make clearings where they could build huts. These villages became bases to return to after hunting, fishing and foraging expeditions. The people who lived in them felt more secure than when they had been constantly on the move, and they began to name themselves after animals that had qualities they admired.

Most of the tribes got on well enough with their neighbours, and at particular times of the year they would join together to feast, sing and dance. It was at one of these celebrations that a boy from the Wolf people fell in love with the daughter of the chief of the Swan people. At earlier feasts he'd hardly noticed her, just one of a group of girls who hung around braiding each others' hair, dancing together and giggling a lot. Now, suddenly, she seemed to be the most beautiful creature he had ever seen. During the dancing he had managed to get quite close to her, but she had looked past him, into the smoke of the fire, and he imagined that she was dreaming of marrying the son of a chief.

When there was a break in the dancing, the old story-teller sat by the edge of the fire, and began the tale of the Magic Monster Bear:

In this family there were three hunters, and they were famous for never giving up on their prey. Once they were on the trail, they would hunt to the final kill. They had a dog called Four Eyes, whose eyes had black circles round them. Four Eyes was able to see tracks that were invisible to humans.

A message reached the hunters that a nearby village was being menaced by a massive bear. The children no longer played out in the woods, houses were barred, and when the villagers woke in the morning they found giant paw prints in the earth around their homes.

The hunters set off through the woods, with Four Eyes running beside them. They were determined to help the people of the threatened village.

As they got closer to the village, they noticed that there was no sign of any animals among the trees, and no bird song.

They came to an old pine tree. High up on its trunk were gashes where a great beast had stood on its hind legs and ripped into the bark with its claws. The first hunter tried to touch the claw marks with the tip of his spear, but he couldn't reach. 'This isn't an ordinary bear,' he said. 'This is the Magic Monster Bear.'

'If that's true,' said the second hunter, 'it could be good for us. I've never seen the Magic Monster Bear myself, but I've spoken to old people who have. They say that the Magic Monster Bear is a treacherous creature; he can creep up on you and eat you without you even realising that he's there. But, once you've spotted his tracks, he's forced to flee.'

The third hunter said, 'I hope we've brought plenty of food. It sounds like this is going to be a long hunt.'

The hunters arrived at the village. It was a sad-looking place. In the very centre, where a fire once burned day and night, there was a pile of grey ash. The doors of the huts were barred, and there was no sign of the women, the children and the old people. The men kept guard; with clubs and spears in their hands, they eyed the fringes of the forest.

The head man came forward to speak to the hunters. Yes, he said, there was certainly a bear. Even though none of the villagers had seen it yet, every morning, when they woke, they found giant paw prints in the earth around their huts, and when they looked up they saw that the trees were scarred with huge claw marks. They were preparing for the day when the bear would come out of the forest in broad daylight.

'We don't think this is an ordinary bear,' said the first hunter. 'We think it's the Magic Monster Bear. But don't worry, we'll track it down and kill it. We never give up on our prey.'

'We've got Four Eyes the dog,' said the second hunter. 'He can see tracks that are invisible to humans.'

'Do you have any food, and somewhere we could lie down and rest before we start the hunt? And maybe a couple of pretty girls to keep us company?' said the third hunter.

'He's just joking,' said the first hunter. And they set off to find the bear.

They hunted for days, and there was no sign of any bear, though all the time they had the feeling that they were being watched from within the woods. The third hunter had brought along some food, some deer meat and fat, pounded together with berries, which he was keeping in a pouch. When he emptied the contents of the pouch into his hand, white, wriggling worms slid out. The Magic Monster Bear had put a spell on the food. But the third hunter was so hungry that he ate the worms anyway.

As the hunt continued, the air became colder. At the end of a long day, when the three hunters were beginning to lose hope of ever finding the bear, Four Eyes yelped. He'd spotted tracks. Immediately the bear appeared close by, with its long sharp claws, its long sharp teeth, and its burning red eyes. It was running away from the hunters. Its fur was white. It looked like a ghost.

Four Eyes kept close to the bear, snapping at its heels, and the hunters followed as best they could. After a while the third hunter got fed up with running. He faked a fall and pretended to twist his ankle so the other two had to pick him up and carry him and his spear. It was hard for them to keep going with the extra weight, and the bear was pulling ahead, up the mountain slopes. Then it turned and looked down at Four Eyes. It reared up on its hind legs, opened its mouth, and bared its long sharp teeth.

'I'm fine now,' said the third hunter. 'Let me down.' As soon as he was back on his feet he grabbed his spear, let out a yell, and ran off after the bear. The bear turned and took the mountain slope, with Four Eyes and the third hunter close behind.

The other two hunters watched them disappear into the clouds at the top of the mountain. They were exhausted with carrying their companion, but they kept on the trail, climbing higher and higher until it grew dark and they could no longer see the ground beneath their feet. Eventually, in the distance, they saw a light and, when they got closer, there was the third hunter. He had already killed and butchered the bear. Its meat was turning on a spit over a fire, and the white fat dripped down, sizzling on the embers.

'Hey boys, where have you been?' he said. 'Come and sit down. Eat some of the bear meat I've killed and cooked for you.'

When the feast was over, even the third hunter was more than full.

'Look,' said the first hunter, pointing downwards. There was no sign of the mountain. All around them were glittering points of light. They hadn't noticed that the bear had run right up off the top of the mountain and high into the sky. They were sitting among the stars.

'Look there,' said the second hunter. The bear's bones were slowly coming together; muscle and sinew, flesh and fur formed on them. The bear stood up and lumbered away.

'Come on!' shouted the third hunter. He grabbed his spear and set off in pursuit, followed by Four Eyes and the other two hunters.

And the hunters are still up there in the sky, chasing the Magic Monster Bear. There are four stars that make the body of the bear, and following the bear are three more stars – the hunters. And if you look closely and you have really sharp eyes, you can see that the middle hunter is actually two stars. One of them is Four Eyes the dog.

As the year begins to grow old, and the hunt crosses the sky, the bear turns upside down, and people say, 'The lazy hunter has killed the bear.' The bear's blood drips down on to the trees and turns the leaves red. Then the dripping fat falls on the grass and turns it white.

When spring comes round the bear turns over, its bones come together, and it starts to run, and the hunt continues until the following autumn, when the feast begins again.

※

After the boy heard the story of the Magic Monster Bear, it was plain to him what he should do. Early the next morning he took his spear and his bow and arrows, and a pouch with deer meat in, and set off into the forest. He planned to kill an animal, something big like the bear in the story, take it to the chief's daughter and throw it down on to the ground in front of her.

'Now,' he would say, 'see what I've caught and killed just for you. Don't you think I'm a fine hunter?' The chief's daughter would fall in love with him and a marriage would soon take place.

The boy hunted all day, going deeper and deeper into the forest, and further and further away from the huts of the Wolf people. He heard rustlings in the undergrowth and saw distant shapes that might have been large animals, but as the sun began to set and the forest shadows lengthened he knew that he was going to catch nothing, and that he would have to spend the night there, because he was too far from home to find his way back safely in the darkness. He climbed high up into the branches of a tree, making sure that he wasn't sharing it with a lynx. He shook the food, a ball of venison, fat and berries, out of his pouch and ate it, listening to the wolves howling in the distance. Then he closed his eyes and went to sleep.

While he slept, the boy had a dream. The first thing he dreamed was a sound like nothing he had heard before; it was as if the wind was singing. In the dream it was first light. He climbed to the bottom of the tree and saw that there was a path leading deeper into the forest. He followed the path until it opened out into a clearing. In the middle of the clearing was a massive pine tree, and sitting on an old hollow branch of the tree was an eagle, which was pecking holes in the branch. A wind blew through the clearing into the hollow branch, and out of the holes that the eagle had pecked, and that was how the beautiful sound was made.

In the morning the boy woke and climbed down the tree, and there was a path, just like the one in his dream. He followed the path into the heart of the forest until he came to a clearing. In the middle of the clearing was a massive pine tree. The boy broke an old, hollow branch from the tree and took it back to the clearing where the Wolf people had their huts. He spent all day making sure the branch was completely hollow, and cutting holes in it with his flint knife, in the same places that the dream eagle had pecked. Somehow he knew where to carve a notch in the end of the branch, so that when he blew down it, it whistled; and somehow he knew that if he put his fingers on the holes and lifted them up and put them down again while he blew, the branch would make a sound like the wind singing.

When evening came, the boy took his singing branch and went through the forest until he came to the edge of the clearing where the Swan people had their huts. He stood there, among the shadows, put the end of the branch to his lips and blew. The sound of the wind singing drifted across the clearing until it came to the hut that the chief's daughter shared with her family. She was ready to go to sleep, but when she heard the beautiful sound she had to find out where it was coming from. She crept out of the hut and walked through the darkness until she came face to face with the boy, who was playing just for her. And – the story says – when she looked into his eyes she fell instantly in love with him.

Not long after that, there was a great feast, and the boy from the Wolf tribe was married to the daughter of the chief of the Swan people. When the old chief, the girl's father, died, the young man became chief in his place. He did well enough, but he knew there was something else he could do better, so one day he handed over the job to one of his wife's brothers, and set out into the woods to collect old, hollow branches from the trees. Each one he turned into a wind singer, and each had its own particular song – and so he became the first flute maker. Word of his talents spread, and people travelled for long distances, sometimes hundreds of miles, to trade for his flutes. They brought finely woven cloth, stone axe heads, jet beads that he in turn could exchange for food and clothing for his family. The flutes became so popular that the flute-maker trained his whole family to make the instruments. Flutes were made and were taken away by their proud new owners, but there was one flute he would never part with. It was the very first wind singer, the instrument inspired by the eagle that pecked holes in the hollow branch of a massive pine tree. Every evening, after the making was finished, the man who had fallen in love with the chief's daughter, all those years before, would take out that first flute and play for his wife and children, and later for his grandchildren and their children too. And when he'd taken his very last breath, the flute was placed in his hands, a companion to go with him to the next world.

THE HARPER OF LOCHBUIE

Clan chieftains were once great patrons of the arts. They would employ poets, pipers, singers, and clarsairs; the clarsairs in particular – skilled players of the harp – were often figures with an international reputation, who moved from one post to another and were treated more like guests than servants. The tradition eventually went into decline, and the last clan harper played his final *puirt* some time in the early decades of the eighteenth century. This story took place a hundred years or so before then.

Loch Buie is a sea loch on the south side of Mull, sheltering the settlement of Lochbuie at its head. It's much more easily reached by water than overland. The Laird of Lochbuie had a son who was a bright boy and loved playing out of doors. There was a girl, the daughter of a widow who was one of Lochbuie's servants, and she and the boy were always together, running through the woodlands and up the slopes, swimming in the water at the edge of the loch. At evening they would walk along the shore holding hands, and they sometimes talked of getting married, as childhood sweethearts do.

When he was twelve years old, Lochbuie's son was sent to France, to get a gentleman's education. As time passed, the girl grew up to become a beautiful young woman, a trusted servant in Lochbuie's hall. Young men of all classes tried to flirt with her, and some asked her to marry them, but she gave them no attention because she was convinced that young Lochbuie would come back and claim her hand.

Around the time that the girl first began to doubt the inevitability of her loved one's return, Lochbuie decided to employ a harper. This man had worked all over Europe – in Rome, Paris, Dublin, Canterbury, Cologne – playing for kings and princesses, bishops and warlords. When he was a young man the itinerant life had suited him very well. He loved travel, and he loved playing music, and the job brought as much good living as he could cope with. But now he was getting older; travelling tired him, and he was thinking that he should consider settling down, perhaps even getting married. This quiet spot by the loch side on the island of Mull seemed just the place to rest and wonder about these possibilities.

The harper settled happily into his new post. Life dawdled along; there was plenty of fresh game to eat, and the wine was surprisingly good for such a remote location. The blacksmith was able to fashion new harp pins and brass strings if they were needed, and there were skilled joiners to make any small repairs to his clarsach. Unlike some other patrons, Lochbuie seemed to enjoy the music, and even encouraged the harper to create new compositions, something he hadn't done for a long time. What pleased the harper more than anything else was that, whenever he played, he would notice a pretty servant girl listening like a bright bird, with her head cocked to one side, quite plainly enchanted. Experience had taught him how easily music could stir amorous feelings. Sometimes this had got him into trouble – he recalled one early morning when he needed to flee Padua in a hurry – but he foresaw no trouble here, just the smallest possibility that love of the music might grow into affection for the player.

Shy passing words between the harper and the girl became conversations about anything from the patience of the heron, to how a face or a way of walking might inspire a melody. The two of them were often seen out walking together and, though a few cruel words were spoken by gossips, most people were delighted when the marriage was announced, then celebrated with a great feast, and with plenty of music and dancing. The couple set up in a cottage on the estate, and it was plain that they were very happy together. Both continued to work for Lochbuie. The girl was a good cook and kept her husband well fed, the lively conversations continued between them, and every evening, before they went to bed, the old harper would play, while his young wife closed her eyes, and dreamed of all the wonderful things that he had described to her from his travels – the golden, painted palaces, the dancing girls lithe as hinds, the rivers broad as deserts.

They married in the autumn and, the following spring, the harper had been asked by Lochbuie to play at the wedding of a relative who lived in the north of the island. His wife got permission to put aside her duties for a few days and go with her husband, and they set off on a bright morning in early April up Gleann a' Chaiginn Mhòir, the Glen of the Big Rocky Pass. At any time of the year the Highland weather can change abruptly. Around noon on this particular day, which had begun so well, a cold wind blew white cloud in from the west and, as they climbed higher, a few flakes of snow started to fall. By the end of the afternoon, with the light beginning to fade, the harper and his wife were struggling through a blizzard. The girl had set out in the lightest spring clothes, completely unprepared for the return of winter weather, and even her husband's cloak around her shoulders couldn't keep out the cold.

By the time they reached a cave, high up in the mountains, the harper was wondering in desperation how he could make his wife warm. He had the means of making fire, a flint and steel, and some dry moss, but nothing to burn. There were no trees or even bushes growing in the pass, and just a few twigs, brought in by nesting birds, on the floor of the cave. He gathered the twigs together and made a fire beneath them. He unpacked his harp, picked up a stone and began to break up the instrument, then fed the pieces to the fire. The sound box of the harp had been carved out of a single piece of sycamore, and there was soon a good blaze going. The harper and his wife huddled close to the fire, hoping it would keep burning until dawn. They had some bannocks and cheese, which they ate, and then they sat without speaking, looking into the flames.

Late in the night, after hours of staring at the embers of the burnt harp, the girl first, and then the man, heard the sound of a horse's hooves coming through the racket of the wind. The horse halted near the mouth of the cave, the rider dismounted, and a young man came in. He greeted them, and sat down on the other side of the fire. He told them they were unfortunate to be in such a place on a night like this, and how lucky it was that he had a flask with him. The young man handed the brandy to the harper's wife. She took a sip from the silver neck and her eyes sparkled in the fire's light. The harper himself drank, then handed the brandy back to the young man, but the young man told him to hold on to it. He took a few more sips, and said that it was good brandy, as good as any he had tasted in France.

As the young man and the girl talked quietly, the harper fell asleep. When he opened his eyes there was enough daylight coming into the cave for him to see that the night's fire was now grey ash. He sat up stiffly and looked around; there was no sign of either his wife or the young man. The harper stood and went to the cave's entrance. In the snow he saw two sets of footprints going a short way, a disturbance as their owners mounted the horse, and the hoof prints of the horse itself going back down the pass.

Lochbuie's son had finally returned to claim his childhood sweetheart, and he had found her in a cave high up in the mountains, in a pass which is still called Mam an Tiompain, the Pass of the Harp. The harper turned and looked back at the remains of the fire, and said, '*Is mairg an losg mi an tiompan dhuit.*'

'What a fool I was to burn my harp for you,' is still the proverbial phrase to use when a favour goes unrequited.

FIFE

SHEILA KINNINMONTH

SHEILA KINNINMONTH has been a professional story-teller for over ten years. Being born and brought up with the stories and traditions of the Kingdom of Fife gave her a passion for folklore and folk tales. During a career in education, she was able indulge this passion and share stories at every opportunity, honing her skills and expanding her knowledge with the help of the Scottish Storytelling Centre and the story-tellers she met there. Having retired from education, she now spends her time sharing tales with audiences of all ages in a wide range of settings throughout Scotland. She is actively involved with two storytelling clubs, Blether Tay-gither based in Dundee, and Langspoon tales based in south Fife, collaborating with other storytellers to take storytelling performances and workshops to many annual events and festivals throughout Tayside and Fife.

BUFF BAREFOOT

I first heard of Buff Barefoot many years ago from an elderly relative at a family gathering. I was told she was a ghost who haunted an old mansion house near where he lived. But apart from the story of distinctive footsteps and occasional glimpses of a young woman, no more was forthcoming. When researching *Fife Folk Tales*, I came across a mention of her again in Volume VII of the Folklore Society's *County Folklore* published in 1912 and again in James Wilkie's 1931 volume of *Bygone Fife*. Still no real information, but there was mention of John Jack's *History of St Monance*. It was here I found her story and this story is my reshaping of that story.

❖

One night a tall dark figure wrapped in a black cloak, his face concealed by a hood, was seen carrying a basket on the road from Newark Castle to St Monans. The season was winter. There was no moon. The only light was that of the stars shining on the sea. He deviated neither to the left nor the right till he reached his destination. The basket was left on the doorstep of the tavern near the harbour kept by a certain Grizel Miller, the first brewer and inn-keeper to have existed in Netherton of St Monans. The figure rapped on the door and having done so, disappeared into the gloom.

Grizel had been expecting some supplies for her house so thought that the covered basket contained these, but hearing the visitor retreat called out, 'Wait! I'll get you your baw-bees.' Getting no answer she plucked the basket from the steps, locked the door once again and set it down in a corner of the kitchen. It was late, so she didn't look inside right away but sat down by the fire, thinking it seemed strange that the messenger hadn't waited. All was quiet except for the crackling of the logs in the fire. Suddenly she heard a strange noise and she imagined she saw something move in the shadows where the flames of the fire flickered on the wall. The supernatural was always lurking on the edges of folk's minds in those days so Grizel called fearfully to her niece who, hearing the tremble in her aunt's voice, came in with an open bible already in her hand.

The shrill cry of an infant came from the basket as she entered.

'Lord be with us lassie, it's a bairn! Do you think it's a fairy changeling?' the old lady asked as she lifted the basket to the table and removed the cover, fearing that the fairies had left one of their imps, despite there being no new-borns to take in exchange. But this was no imp! It was a newborn bairn, a fine wee lassie dressed in the best of clothes and with a bag of gold hidden in the blanket.

'In all the wide world what does this mean?' asked Grizel. 'This is no common bairn but probably a mistake of the laird. We'll take the bairn and call it our ain.' So here the matter rested for the night.

The next day the laird from Grangemuir visited the inn as he often did for his amusement because there he was able to catch up on all the goings-on of the district. This time, though, the marvellous basket was all that was being talked about and he listened with intense interest.

'It's a braw fair-skinned bairn, sir, and not that unlike yourself if my een dinna deceive me.'

'Wheest Grizel!', replied the laird. 'You're surely daft!'

'No, sir, I'm not that daft. It has the very same black een that you have.'

'No more of your nonsense. Bring me some ale.'

'Aye, aye,' says Grizel. 'But there's much worse can come to your house than a braw wee bairn, ye ken.'

Grizel was much enamoured with the child and took it upon herself to raise her and keep her from danger both real and imagined by concealing, within the folds of her garments, a huge lammer bead, a bead made of the finest amber, because it is well known in the East Neuk for its mystic ability to protect defenceless children from any fairy influence.

The seasons passed and the little mysterious foundling grew up as fair as a lily, hardy and strong but more genteel than the maids around her. It was noted, almost with surprise, that she followed the practice of the class in which she had been raised by taking a dislike to footwear and going without shoes. What Christian name she was given has been long forgotten but because of this habit, she was known in St Monans as Buff Barefoot.

Seventeen years passed, each year celebrated with a party at the laird's home, Grangemuir House, to which all were invited, common folk and gentry alike. This year after the celebration the girl was returning from helping a much inebriated guest home when a huge Newfoundland dog bounded towards her. At first she shrank with terror from the hound but when it lay down at her feet, gazing at her with its big brown eyes, she realised it meant her no harm. As she reached to stroke it, the dog gently took a hold of her skirt with its teeth and pulled as if saying, 'Come with me.' When it ran off, she followed and then the whole mystery unfolded. A fine ship dashed to pieces on the rocks, the shore strewn with the wreck. The captain, a fine young man and sole survivor of the catastrophe, thrown up on the beach and left so entangled with the wreck by the receding tide as to make it impossible to free himself. The dog ran and licked his face and together girl and dog were able to release the sailor and take him back to her foster mother's home, where he was welcomed and given the necessary treatment his condition needed. It turned out that this mariner was in fact a long lost nephew of Grizel, the family having been scattered to the four corners of the Empire. When he saw the beautiful young girl who had rescued him from certain death, he fell completely in love with her and Grizel could see that the girl returned that love. Having been duped by a sailor herself in the past and having the feeling that this girl, though penniless, was of high descent and a match for a baron or some other titled suitor, Grizel arranged for the stranger to go live with her brother. Here he stayed until his affairs were settled and then because he had lost everything in the shipwreck he was sent off on a trading voyage to recoup his lost fortune.

Meanwhile the mansion at Grangemuir was visited by a distant relative of the laird. This visitor was in fact a border freebooter who had amassed a fortune by plunder and criminal acts and who had no conscience or heart. He was introduced to the beauty of St Monans and Grizel's tavern was much visited by him so he could meet her. But she refused all his attentions.

The day was now near when the sailor was to return to claim his bride and the border raider, learning this, determined to take his place. He discovered how letters came and went between the lovers then intercepted a message asking Buff to welcome back her lover in the moonlight beneath St Mary's tree on the Doocot Hill. She told her foster mother that she was going to keep the tryst and she did. Scarcely had she time to reach the spot than St Monans was roused by shrieks and pistol shots. The sailor reached the spot first and seeing the figure of a man running off, followed him. The villagers, some still in their nightclothes, found Buff Barefoot dying on the ground and far off in the distance a fleeing figure. He was pursued and, stumbling in the unfamiliar landscape, was overtaken and recognised as the sailor from over the sea. The freebooter was nowhere to be seen. The sailor was taken and locked up in a dungeon at Newark Castle to await his fate. The real villain was eventually overcome with remorse. His wild life in the Borders had troubled him little but now the ghosts of the past peopled his dreams and his waking hours alike, so he confessed before finally finding a suicide's grave.

From the moment of her death the spirit of Buff Barefoot haunted Grangemuir House. Every night the sound of bare feet running through its rooms and along its passages disturbed the sleep of the household. There were some who saw as well as heard. For a century it is said that only those impervious to fear stayed at the mansion. Eventually it was abandoned. Another house was built a little way off but not a scrap of masonry from the old house was used in the building of the new in case the ghost should follow.

THE WITCH OF FIFE

A popular and well-known tale amongst Scottish storytellers, this is a story I have known forever. It is based on a comic narrative poem written, in Scots, by Scottish poet James Hogg (1770-1835), sometimes known as the Ettrick Shepherd since as a young man he worked as a shepherd and farmhand. Largely self-taught, he was a friend of many of the great writers of his day such as Walter Scott and William Wordsworth.

❖

Once, a long time ago in the Kingdom of Fife, there lived a gudeman and his wife. The old man was a quiet and hardworking soul but his wife was so skeerie and flighty that the neighbours used to nudge each other and whisper that they feared she might be a witch. And her husband was afraid that it might be true because she had a curious habit of disappearing in the evening and staying out all night and when she did come back in the morning she looked quite white and tired, as if she had travelled far or worked hard. Try as he might to watch her carefully and find out where she went and what she did he never managed to do so because she always slipped out of the door while he wasn't looking, and before he had reached it to follow her she had vanished completely.

Eventually, one day, the husband decided it was time he knew, so he asked her right out if she was a witch. But his blood ran cold when, without hesitation, she answered that she was and if he promised not to let anyone know, the next time she went out on one of her adventures she would tell him all about it. Well the old man agreed because he thought it was only right that a husband should know all about what his wife got up to.

He didn't have long to wait because the very next week it was a new moon and the time when witches like to venture out. That very night his wife vanished and didn't return until daybreak.

When he asked her where she had been, it was with great excitement and pleasure that she told her story. She had met four other companions in the old kirkyard where they had mounted branches of the green bay tree and stalks of hemlock, which had immediately turned into horses carrying them, swift as the wind, over the country, hunting the foxes, the weasels and the owls. Then they had swum the loch and come to the top of the Lomond Hills, where they had dismounted and drunk beer made in no earthly brewery from little horn cups made by no mortal hand. Then a wee man had appeared from under a great mossy stone with a tiny set of bagpipes under his arm and played such wonderful music that, at the sound of it, the very fish jumped out of the loch below, and the stoats crept out of their holes, and the crows and herons came and sat on the trees in the darkness just to listen. The witches danced until they were so tired that they could hardly hang on to their horses on the way home.

The gudeman listened to this long story in silence, shaking his head from time to time, and when it was finished all that he said was, 'And what good has all that dancing done you? Would you not have been better at home in bed with your dear little bairns and me?'

The next new moon saw the wife disappearing again. When she returned this time she told of how she and her friends had taken cockleshells from the beach and turned them into boats and had sailed over the stormy sea to Norway. There they had mounted invisible horses of wind and had ridden over mountains, glens and glaciers until they reached the frozen lands of the Lapps, lying under a cloak of snow. Here all the elves, fairies and mermaids of the North were holding a festival with warlocks, broonies, pixies and even the Phantom Hunters themselves, who are never seen by mortal eyes. The Witches of Fife joined in with the dancing, feasting and singing. She told how the warlock men and weird women had washed them with witch-water, distilled from the moorland dew till their beauty bloomed like the Lapland rose that grows wild in the forest. Then, soft in the arms of the warlock men, they had lain down to sleep. But more importantly, they were taught certain magical words which, when spoken, would carry them through the air and undo all bolts and bars and gain them entry to any place they wanted to be. They had returned home, delighted with the knowledge they had been given.

'You're lying,' cried out the old man, 'you're lying. The ugliest wife on the shores of Fife is bonnier than you! Why would the warlock men lie with you? And what took you to such a cauld land? Would you no' have been warmer at home in bed wi' me?'

But the next time he took a wee bit more notice of what she said, because she told of how they had met in the cottage of one of her friends and how, having heard that the Lord Bishop of Carlisle had a very fine wine cellar, they had each placed a foot on the pan hook over the fire and had spoken the magic words they had learned from the Elves of Lapland. As soon as the words were out of their mouths they disappeared up the chimney like whiffs of smoke and sailed through the air like little clouds to land at the bishop's palace in Carlisle.

There the doors flew open and they went down into the bishop's wine cellar, where they sampled the fine wines, returning to Fife, fine sober old women, by daybreak.

When he heard this the old man took notice. He liked a fine wine himself but it seldom came his way.

'You are a wife to be proud of,' he cried. 'Maybe you could tell me these words? I would like to go and sample the bishop's wine myself.'

'Na, na,' she replied. 'I couldn't do that because you might tell it over again and the whole world would be turned upside down with folk going into each other's houses whenever they pleased.' And although he tried to persuade her with all the soft words he could think of, she wouldn't give up her secret.

But he had a sly side and the thought of the bishop's wine stayed with him, so night after night he visited the other cottages in the hope that he would catch his wife and her friends meeting there. It took a long time but at last his trouble was rewarded. One night they assembled and in low tones, amid chuckles of laughter as they reminded each other of their adventures in Lapland, one by one they climbed onto the sooty hook, repeated the magic words, and disappeared up the lum.

'I can do that too,' he thought, crawling out of his hiding place and running to the fire, where he put his foot on the hook and repeated the magic words he had heard. He too flew up the lum and out into the night air after his wife and her companions. And, as witches never look over their shoulders, he wasn't noticed until they reached the bishop's cellar. They weren't pleased when they discovered he was amongst them but what could they do? They got on with enjoying themselves, sampling the wines as before. But while they just took a little here and a little there, the husband was not so cautious. He drank so much that he was fast asleep on the floor when the time came to leave. Thinking to teach him a lesson, they left him there to be discovered the next morning by the bishop's servants. Much surprised to find him in a locked cellar, he was dragged before the bishop himself, who asked for an explanation. The poor old man was so confused that all he could say was that he came from Fife 'on the midnight wind'. Hearing that, the bishop declared he must be a warlock and ordered him to be burnt alive.

Well the poor man now wished he had minded his own business and stayed at home. But it was too late. He was dragged outside and chained to a great iron stake. Piles of wood were placed around his feet and set alight. As the flames crept up he thought his last hour had come. Just then there was a swish and a flutter of wings and a bird appeared in the sky, swooping down to perch for a moment on the old man's shoulder to whisper in his ear. The old man's heart jumped for joy as he realised this was his wife with her magic words. He called them out and immediately the chains fell away and the old man sailed off into the air, much to the amazement of the crowd. And when he found himself safely at home once more he vowed to leave his wife to her own devices from then on and never try to find out her secrets.

MIDLOTHIAN

LEA TAYLOR

LEA TAYLOR is a professional storyteller working out of Midlothian. She uses traditional tales and local lore to connect people, reflect culture and promote curiosity. Lea gained an MA (Hons) in Scottish Ethnology at Edinburgh University and went on to study a post graduate qualification in Community Education. Lea has worked with all manner of groups, from schools and residential care homes, to hospices, Women's Aid and governmental organisations, and is particularly interested in storytelling and literacy development. Lea has written and performed for national and international audiences, and lives in Midlothian with her husband and son.

AN UNLIKELY AUCTION

This is one of my favourite stories, reported in a broadside some three hundred years ago. The event lends itself to the rich texture of Edinburgh life in an age gone by – assuming that activities such as this don't happen over the internet. Or do they?

If I stand in the middle of Edinburgh's Grassmarket, close my eyes and take in the hustle and bustle of the place, I can almost see the event unfold.

❖

It wasn't as if he was being unreasonable. Every other man he knew had a wife he could come home to, be greeted with a civil smile, a plate of warm food on the table, and a hearth and house in neat and clean order. There was no excuse, there were no children to attend to, yet.

Twice that week he had come home to find his wife, Mary, passed out on the floor. Empty bottles at her side and the house in disarray. As Thomas Guisgan stood over her he nudged her with the toe of his boot. She murmured, opened her bleary eyes and squinted at him before turning her face away, muttering her irritation. Words stumbled out of her mouth as if colliding into each other. He could make no sense of what she was saying but smelt the familiar stench of stale porter.

Bile rose in the back of his throat; anger pure and simple made him gag and gasp. It was one thing to have a slovenly wife, but to have a wife a slave to the porter was too hard to accept. His honour and reputation were at stake and she was beyond his help or tolerance.

He resolved to find a solution, one that would accommodate both of their needs.

Leaving her lying on the cold stone floor, her dark hair fanned out around her, he stepped back out into the night. The crisp air helped to clear his mind as he wandered through the fog, passing shadowy figures. He made his way along the Grassmarket, then up Lady Lawson Street to the auctioneer's office. There was a flicker of light from within. Someone was still there.

His fists beat loudly on the door, perhaps a little overzealous, but better to take it out on the door than elsewhere. The startled clerk put his pen down and shuffled to answer it. Opening cautiously he peered out, 'Sir, I was just about to …'

'I'll not take much of your time.' Guisgan brushed past, bringing the cold night air in with him.

After the formalities had been exchanged, the elderly clerk sat back in his chair and let out a long sigh and made a bridge with his stubby ink-stained fingers.

'Your request is most unusual, but I am sure it can be accommodated. We will, of course, levy our usual fees for our services and rest assured we will attend to all the necessary notices for a …' he hesitates for a second and a smile passes his lips, 'meagre sum.'

Guisgan reached into his pocket, pulled out a small leather purse and tossed the coins on the counter.

'Until Thursday then, Sir.'

'Until Thursday.'

It was an exceptionally large crowd that gathered in the Grassmarket that day. There was an air of expectant anticipation. Several stallholders had pitched their stands closer to the auction house, as if they knew today would be a day for swift trade, and they were not disappointed. By 6 p.m. some two thousand people had gathered and there were more still coming.

Guisgan arrived, feeding the spectacle by leading his wife with a makeshift straw rope tied around her waist and a notice pinned to her bosom with the words 'to be sold by public auction'. The crowd fell silent and shifted uneasily as Guisgan and his forlorn wife, Mary McIntosh, stepped through.

It started off fairly civilly. Mary was made to climb up onto a wee platform so she could be seen above the crowd. It quietened momentarily as a sea of expectant faces took in the scene. Mary was fair of face, her dark hair had been braided and tied up to show her high cheekbones and bright, engaging blue eyes. Her face flushed as she cast her gaze down, making her appear vulnerable and innocent. When the church clock rang out the last of its chimes for six o'clock, the auctioneer took to his lectern, his white hair standing out against the grey evening light. Gavel in hand he struck the desk to gain everybody's attention. He wrestled to be heard above the clamouring crowd; the babbling had risen from hushed tones to a swell of derisive shouts as the mass surged and swayed. He banged his gavel down again and again but the crowd was beginning to jostle and collide as more folk arrived to witness the event.

The bidding started. The first bid came as a shout from the crowd, and a Highland drover stepped through. He looked rough and unshaven, his broad shoulders swathed in a heavy plaid. He stood before the auctioneer, pulled out his purse and said, 'She be a guid like lassie, I will gie ten and twenty shillings for her.' The crowd gave a rousing cheer but his bid was bettered by a stout tinker who bolted up the front, bowling people out of his way. His rich voice rose above the noise.

'She should never go to the Highlands before offering a sixpence.' The crowd laughed indulgently.

Next up came a bid from a Killarney pig jobber, with a mouth as wide as a turnpike gate. His face was red and his eyes looked in opposite directions, and had it not been for the crowd pressing and clamouring against each other it's highly possibly the pig jobber would have fallen flat on his face.

Half-drunk, he offered a further two shillings more given that she was a 'pratty' (or mischievous) woman. By this point the mood of the crowd was beginning to change. Then a brogue maker, having just emerged from an alehouse as drunk as fifty cats in a wallet, stepped forward and hit the Killarney man full on the nose, knocking him out for a good ten minutes.

Standing at close quarters and witnessing the whole thing, Mary McIntosh laughed heartily and the crowd joined in, giving long and incessant cheers. But the scene deteriorated rapidly as bare-knuckle fighting broke out – much of it carried out by women armed with stones. Then, the drunken brogue maker walked up to the auctioneer and knocked him and the lectern down; his mug of claret flowed freely all over the floor.

By this time the neighbourhood women had gathered, all seven hundred of them, and they had a look of militant intent. Initially they stood on the perimeter of the crowd armed with stones, some of which were loaded into stockings or handkerchiefs while others threw them freely. Then they made a general charge through the mob, knocking down everyone that came their way until they finally reached the auctioneer. He cowered behind the lectern, pleading loudly that he should be left alone. The furious women set upon him, scratched and tore at his face in a terrifying manner, screeching at the top of their voices, utterly vexed by the insult the fair sex had received.

The crowd looked on aghast. One women, the wife of a sweep, later described as a true herione, suddenly spied Thomas Guisgan and let vent her anger by pelting him with stones; after all, he was the cause of all the commotion. Above the din her voice could be heard calling him all kinds of vile names, but mostly the words 'contaminated villain' carried across the Grassmarket. Guisgan, who was evidently not known for his gentlemanly airs, retaliated against the assault and punched the wifey smartly between the eyes, leaving them like two October cabbages.

A general battle ensued and, had it not been for police intervention, lives surely would have been lost. After a while the worst of the rammy was quelled and the crowd stood waiting for the auction to recommence.

Once again Mary was brought up before the crowd. At this point an elderly seaman, Jack Tar, stepped forward and indicated his interest while using the words 'well rigged' to describe her. The auctioneer, having suitably recovered from his earlier encounter, took a note of his offer for half a crown, which was more than the previous bidder. But Jack Tar was soon disappointed and his offer topped by a farmer, said to be a widower, who pledged two pounds and five shillings. The sale was agreed and the gavel hit the lectern to confirm the sale.

The farmer led Mary McIntosh away through the crowd to where his horse stood patiently waiting. There he mounted his horse and took Mary up behind him.

They rode away midst the cheers of the populace. There never was another auction of this ilk held again.

❖

For anyone wishing to see the actual broadside it can be found in the National Library of Scotland: Lauriston Catalogue L.C. 1268(092): Sale of Wife.

THE FAIRY BOY OF LEITH

Sounds from the King's Cavern

I am their brusher and beater
I brush the beater for January
Their harps are the birch
I drum the corners, four points
North, South, East and West
I cross the seas to Kings who know best
I cross the skies o'er Kings who know less
I triple paradiddle
I drag up the gates
I roll down the hill
I drag up the gates
I roll down the hill
And when all is still, I slide home.

(Claire Druett, storyteller and poet, 2012)

This is ma story, o' how it came tae be. I dinnae expect ye tae believe it a', but I assure ye it is all true from where a'm standin'. I wis born and bred in Leith, Edinburgh, in the year o' Our Lord 1660. Back then it wis a bustling seaport wi' all manner o' life in an' aboot the docks. I grew up in the squalor o' the tenements. Ma family, like ithers aroond us, lived a hand-tae-mooth existence, particularly so eifter ma faither died. I wis eight year old.

Mither sent me oot early that mornin' tae get some messages. She needed milk fer the bairn, my youngest brither, only six month old an' sick wi' the colic. Rain wis pelting down as the carriages barrelled past. I loved watchin' the posh folk sittin' in them all poker-faced and la-de-da lookin' doon on us 'street urchins'. I used tae wonder whit it would be like tae hae a belly full o' food an' a warm hoose tae bide in. If I'd had a magic wand I'd ha' wished fer a meat pie the size o' ma heid an' a gallon o' ale, but in they days ma wishes were simply that, wishes.

I tapped ma way tae the corner shop. Using two sturdy twigs I played the railings, thrummed at doors, pattered the windae panes, a rhythm wis in ma heid a' just could'nae shake. Life tae me was played oot in rhythmic patterns, even down tae ma eyelid's soundless blink. It all stopped when a passin' coal cart hit a rut in the rood. It made quite a bang sending the horses aff in tae a panic. The cart-man had trouble reining them in, they jerked in their harness this way an' that, scattering bits o' coal across the street. Barely had it hit the floor when all us street bairns went runnin', scrabblin' aboot the cart wheels an' horses hooves, pouncin' on every piece we found. Any lump o' coal wis a welcome treat for the range.

Me an' Frankie O'Dowd spied the same piece, it seemed massive. We both made a dive for it, all elbows and knees. I got there first, but he, bein' bigger than me, prised it oot o' ma fingers. I looked him in the e'e, clenched ma jaw and gritted ma teeth but he wasn'ae gang tae gie it up that easily an' peeled ma fingers back yin by yin. So I bled his neb. We ended up rolling aboot in the gutter, joined by the ither bairns lookin' on, jeerin an' shouting. By then we had lost sicht o' the coal, too intent on blacking each other's een. Mr Muir the shopkeeper grabbed us both by the scruff o' oor necks an' threatened tae knock some sense in tae the pair o' us. I remember yellin' doon the street, 'I'll see yoos later Frankie O'Dowd,' as I watched him disappear doon Junction Street. Only then did I taste blood on my swollen lip.

Ma grazed fingers throbbed wi' pain an' cold. But that didn'ae stop me tapping oot a rhythm. This wis ma favourite thing tae dae, tappin', drummin', thrummin'. If I didn'ae have ony sticks I would use ma fingers. Sometimes I amazed mysel', it's as if ma honds an' fingers had a life o' their ain. Gangin sae fast, a flurry o' activity an' sound.

The main thing I remember aboot that day wis the sound o' drummin' wellin' up frae a distance. It wis faint at first, but got louder and louder. We all ran tae where the sound wis coming from, Frankie O'Dowd too.

That mornin' ma world completely changed. It wis the first time I had ever witnessed a parade like that. It wis braw. The soldiers, all dressed up in their smart uniforms, three abreast marchin' frae a troop ship headin' up the street towards the castle in time tae the pipe and drums. I was transfixed. The sheer beauty o' the drum roll, the snap o' the drumsticks an' the booming big bass drum as the crowd whooped and hollered.

The drummer threw his sticks high in tae the air, let them twirl, then caught them like he wasn'ae even tryin and withoot stopping. He didn'ae miss a step or blink an e'e. It wis then I knew that that wis what I wanted tae dae. Drum withoot missin' a step as though it wis part o' ma being, like breathin' or walkin'. No fae me workin' at the docks as a stevedore, coming hame late an' tired, hands blistered an' back bent double wi' pain. I had nae idea how I wis tae mak this dream a reality either but I kenned deep doon that it wis part o' me.

Later that day, I wis up Carlton Hill, I'd been messin' aboot wi some o' the laddies at The Top o' The Walk. We'd been cheeky tae wan o' the stallholders, stolen a pie an' when chased, scattered like nine pins. I bolted up the steps leading tae Carlton Hill jist as the sun wis gangin' doon. I really should ha' been hame but I kenned that the stall-holder wis probably still aboot, I didn'ae want a skelping so I decided tae wait a bit longer. I sat quietly fer a bit – soon ma fingers were dancin' awa', drumming oot a tune. It sounded great tae me in ma heid. Next thing I knew I wis staring at this wee man, nay taller than ma knee, all dressed in green standin' richt there afore me. He had come through a wee door cut intae the hillside. I'd never noticed it before an' even if you looked really hard it would be hard tae place. The door wis wooden, a nondescript type o' wood, the top o' it arched tae match the curve o' the hill. Fancy markings were carved deep in tae the wood, pretty patterns an' swirls all linked an' looping. No sooner had the evening licht struck the door when the markings appeared tae take on a life o' their ain an' began tae shimmer an' dance.

The wee man took aff his hat an' made a long low bow. His face wis awfae handsome, fine chiselled cheekbones an' arresting emerald green een. I wis momentarily dumb-struck. In a melodious soft voice, he said he wis pleased tae meet me. Even kenned ma name. He enquired as tae whether I wis hungry an' if I would like tae join him an' his friends on the ither side o' the door. Normally I would ha' rin a mile, but strangely ma feet were rooted tae the spot. The door wis opened just a wee bit an' a bricht golden licht flickered frae the ither side. Inside there wis movement, lots o' movement, whirlin' and dancin', the wild an' fun kind. Even more compelling wis the beauti-ful music. A mix o' heavenly bells, pipes, whistles an' fid-dles, all in perfect rhythm an' harmony. Mair excited than afraid, I followed him, bending ma heid an' stooping tae step through the magical door an in tae the licht an' a huge stuccoed room.

Noo I'm back there every Thursday evenin, rain o' shine. Mither has given up trying tae stop me.

'Come hame lad,' she would plead, 'I'm feart for ye'. At first she greeted an' wrung her honds. 'There's nay sich thing as fairies an' elves' son.'

She changed her mind when I told her fortune; the wee folk had gi'en me the gift o' second sicht. I showed her trinkets gi'en tae me by the fairies, craftsmanship like nae ither an' marvellous tae behold.

But best o' all, they schooled me in the art o' drummin'. It wis a dream come true. They said ma passion fer drummin' shone through, so they took me in tae their musical vaults, gave me a drum, showed me how tae play it wi' and from the hairt. I learned tae play, play onything I cared tae. Like the sound o' raindrops or a tricklin' stream, applause, a jig, a reel, a strathspey, even cart wheels traivellin' across a cobbled street. And in exchange for this gift, I wis tae play for them on Thursday nichts. A small price tae pay don't ye think?

They held wonderful parties. Tables loaded wi' all kinds o' sumptuous foods, the likes o' which I had ne'er seen or tasted before. Then there wis the wine, the sweetest ye could ever imagine, like nectar frae the gods an' ne'er ending jugs o' it. And always, they were the kindest and most beautiful beings I had e'er met. Sometimes we would travel tae France or even Holland for these parties an' be back afore sunrise. Ne'er a dull moment.

At hame, in the world ootside the hill, word got roond that I wis drummin' fer the wee folk. Naebody seemed to question it. Sometimes folk would pass by then stop an' point – 'Look, it's the fairy boy o' Leith.'

Yin day, a lady frae the lodging hoose jist a couple o' streets away frae me, asked me if I would come an' speak tae yin o' her lodgers, a Captain George Burton, he wis a merchant seaman. She said he wis impressed wi' ma drummin'.

I turned up the next day, jist eifter breakfast. I wis shown in tae the drawing room. Captain Burton wis there wi' some o' his cronies. They seemed friendly enough, asked lots o' questions aboot the wee folk, ma drummin', where I'd visited wi' them an' some o' the important sights there. Then they asked aboot ma family an' the school I attended.

The captain seemed interested but no entirely convinced aboot the fairy folk, so I used the gift they gie'd me an' told him his fortune; tae prove the efficacy o' ma powers I told the captain that he had had twa wives, saw the forms o' them sitting on his shoulders. Both handsome women, wan o' the women asked me tae tell the captain that she had twa bairns oot o' wedlock afore she married him. It wis something that he already kenned but wis shocked wi' ma insight.

Time wis slipping by an' I needed tae be away, up the hill. The captain an' his acquaintances tried tae talk me in tae staying longer – I didn'ae want tae tarry an' found an excuse tae leave. They fetched me back again an' tried tae bar the door. It wis a futile attempt, naethin' would hold me back frae ma important assignation. The wee folk were no tae be kept waitin' – an' certainly no by me.

Mony years have passed since then. Three days in fairy land equate to seven years in oors. I hear tell I'm a legend noo, the Fairy Boy o' Leith. Ma story survived long aifter I left, for now I bide behind those beautifully carved doors, hidden tae all but the fairy folk, up on Carlton Hill an' I could'nae give twa figs whether ye believe me or no, fer now I march tae a different drum.

EAST LOTHIAN

TIM PORTEUS

TIM PORTEUS loves sharing the wonderful world of folklore, mythology and legend, but he has also developed an interest in collecting and telling more modern urban tales, as well as personal family stories and reminiscences. As a father of five (four daughters, one son), Tim is fully aware of the importance and power of stories for children. He likes to engage his audience and involve them in the story. He sometimes mixes his storytelling with other creative art forms such as music, murals, poetry and film making. Tim is qualified in Community Education and uses storytelling with vulnerable and marginalised groups to enhance self-belief and confidence, assisting people to create their own cultural identities.

WEE SHORT-HOGGERS
OF WHITTINGHAME

Nobody saw her as she huddled secretly under the trees. She had managed to find a place in the wood away from the road, and from the fields. The pains in her body were near unbearable as she knelt, gripping the ground and doing her best to muffle her screams of pain.

She knew she must give birth as silently as possible, she must not be discovered. It was her shame to bear and she'd concealed it for nine months. The man whom she had loved and trusted had disowned her. He was free just to walk away and have nothing more to do with her.

But as the child grew inside her, she knew that because she was unmarried she faced public humiliation and rejection. And so she had concealed the evidence of what she was made to believe was her sin.

It hadn't been easy. She'd worn extra clothing to fool suspicious eyes. She'd worked in the fields as usual. Even still, she was sure some suspected. And now her baby was coming. If she was heard, then all would have been in vain, her life would be ruined. She was in a desperate situation, and her desperation gave her the strength to hide her cries.

And there, under the arching embrace of an old oak tree, she gave birth to her wee baby boy. She cradled him, but he began to cry. She wrapped him tightly in her shawl, rocking to and fro, singing him a lullaby. His mother's tears streamed down her face and fell onto his head, baptising him.

Then a new pain gripped her body. It wasn't a physical pain, but she felt it nonetheless. The trees and birds were the only witnesses to her agony. Soon her son had stopped crying. She let out a howl of grief and guilt, yet it was a silent scream, except within her soul. She carefully unfurled her tiny son from her arms, and kissed him on his forehead. Then she lay his naked and lifeless body on the ground.

She dug furiously with her hands, finding a place between the roots of the tree where her son could rest. And there she lay him, in a cradle of earth. She knelt over him, saying a prayer, asking God to forgive her and pleading that her child be accepted into heaven.

And then in a frenzy she covered him with soil and dirt, with a blanket of leaves and twigs to hide his presence.

She stood and wiped her face. It was done. She now had to return to the fields, and pretend nothing had happened. It was vital she didn't return here, for she could be found out. She must be strong.

In all this she forgot one thing. She forgot to give her son a name.

It was a few years after this that the weeping was first heard. It came from the woods between the kirk and the fields. It was the crying of a young child, but no child was seen.

Then, one evening, it was heard on the road to Stenton. It was the ghostly sound of a young boy crying. Soon afterwards, some farmhands heard the wailing and to their horror they saw a ghostly apparition of a young boy sitting on a wall on the edge of the wood.

He was weeping and holding his head in his hands.

The ghostly young lad threatened nobody, but his presence in the neighbourhood caused people to feel afraid. They would run from him or change direction as soon as they heard or saw him. One person at least knew who this distraught spirit was, but she dared not tell.

It was, of course, the spirit of the wee boy laid to rest in the woods of Whittinghame. His soul could not enter heaven, for he had no name. And so the wee lad's spirit was condemned to wander the woods and lanes of Whittinghame, lamenting his nameless state.

And then, one morning, a local 'drunken blellum' was staggering along the road. He zigzagged along the path, as the alcohol was still affecting his ability to walk straight. He sang an undecipherable tune to himself, and was not too drunk to notice the pleasant morning air, and enjoy the sunrise.

Then he suddenly saw the ghost of the wee nameless boy sitting on a wall, looking forlorn and sad. The drunk man stopped and stared at the wee ghost. As he stood, he swayed to and fro as if about to fall flat on his face. But he was studying the sad face on the boy, and felt for him. He noticed the boy had bare feet and the way the shadow was falling upon him made it look like he was wearing footless stockings.

And so the drunk man raised his arms and his voice, and called out cheerfully, 'Hoo's a' wi ye this morning, Short Hoggers?' In an instant the wee ghost's demeanour changed. Someone had actually talked to him, and what's more, had given him a name.

The wee ghost jumped for joy. Now he finally had a name! He leaped off the wall and skipped away, calling out happily to himself, 'Oh weel's me noo! I've gotten a name. They ca me Short-Hoggers o' Whittinghame!'

And so it must be assumed that this name was accepted for entry into the other world, for after his encounter with the kindly drunk man, the wee ghost was never seen again.

THE HOLY PRINCESS
OF EAST LOTHIAN

There can hardly be a more iconic image of East Lothian than Traprain Law. This great volcanic hill dominates the surrounding countryside, and despite a slice being removed by twentieth-century mining operations, it has lost none of its power to impress.

On its broad summit was once a great fortress, known as Dunpelder or Dunpender, home to the great Celtic tribe called the Gododdin (known to the Romans as the Votadini). The head of this tribe was called King Loth (or Lot). Such was his power and prestige that the name Lothian is said to be derived from his name. He was the brother-in-law of the legendary King Arthur.

And so in choosing a husband for his daughter, Thenew, he decided upon what he considered a suitable match.

'You shall marry Prince Owain,' commanded Loth, for he was a prince from the Celtic kingdom of Rheged, a suitable match that would also enhance Loth's position.

But Thenew felt no affection for the prince. 'Father, I beg you, I do not wish to marry him,' pleaded Thenew.

Soon her pleadings grew into defiance. Her refusal to obey his will enraged King Loth. If he could not control his own daughter, how could he be respected as a king and leader of men! He must teach her a lesson, one in which she would be glad to marry a man of status like Owain.

And so he banished her from her fortress home and forced her to live with a family of swineherds, by the Lammermuir Hills. She would live amongst the muck and dirt of a lowly family, far from the reverence of her royal position. This humiliation would teach her the meaning of life! Soon she would be begging to be freed from such a lowly existence, and agree to marry Owain.

But in that muck and dirt amongst the swine she found a new peace within her heart. She had become a Christian, and to live the simple life of a poor peasant was no hardship for her. What is more, she was in love with the son of the family who looked after her. He loved her dearly in return and when her father's spies watched her she could not hide her happiness. She felt not poor, but richer than she had ever been.

The king's plan was not working! He smashed his hand on the table when given the news of his daughter's joy. And Owain's anger at being rejected fed dark thoughts. 'Take her anyway,' he was advised, 'and once you have taken her she will be yours regardless of her will.'

Her happiness and contented spirit were too much to bear for the men who wanted to control her. So Owain resolved to take her by force. Like a fox he crept in the darkness close to the swineherd's home, in disguise as a woman. He waited for the moment Thenew was alone. Then he raped her. But his violence didn't break her for she still refused to submit to his will.

'You still choose to live amongst the swine?' Owain sneered.

'Even the swine are better than you can ever be,' replied Thenew defiantly.

But soon after, her belly began to swell and the king's spies reported that she was with child. This was a dishonour that King Loth could not tolerate. He brought Thenew back to his fortress. He would listen to nothing she said. Her dishonourable state was plain for all to see.

He sentenced her to death by stoning! Yet no one wanted to be held directly responsible for the death of this young princess, no one wanted to cast the first stone. But the sentence must be carried out, the king's honour and authority were at stake.

And so the stone that would kill her would be the cliff that plunged from the fortress. She was placed upon a cart, which was then taken to the edge. She closed her eyes and prayed, for forgiveness for herself, but also for her father and those who had done her wrong.

The cart was then pushed over the cliff edge by a group of chosen warriors. This way, no one man could be said to have caused her death. Tears were shed by many at the sight, and few could bear to watch.

As the cart plunged down the cliff it was smashed and broken on the rocks, finally coming to a crashing halt over 300 feet below. A group of Thenew's friends waiting at the base of the cliff clenched their chests with horror at the sight of the now crumpled and destroyed chariot, under which lay Thenew. They knew her body must be broken and bloodied, and nobody could have survived such a dreadful crash. They just hoped that her end had been quick.

But then, unbelievably, Thenew emerged. Both she and her unborn child were alive! Her friends fell to their knees and gave thanks to God. They helped Thenew from the wreckage and she prayed with them.

The pole from the cart splintered away and buried itself into the ground like a giant spear. From where it pierced the ground, a spring gushed forth. A holy well was now at the base of the rock.

'What dark magic is this?' cried her father's advisors.

'It is witchcraft,' said the king.

'No sire, a miracle from God!' proclaimed her friends.

'Very well,' said the king to his daughter, 'if this be your God and he wishes to let you and your child live, then I will set you adrift on the sea, and let your God save you.'

And so she was taken to Aberlady Bay, then known as 'the river mouth of the stench' because of the fish thrown from the fishermen's boats. From here she was placed in a coracle, a small round canoe, made of hide. She shuddered with fear as her small craft was pulled from the shore and taken out to sea, then set adrift on the outgoing tide.

The tiny vessel drifted towards the open sea, the water lapping at Thenew's feet as she desperately tried to avoid capsizing. She frantically scooped the water with her hands, but the land began to vanish and the water grew darker, and the coracle began to sink.

She approached the Isle of May, but she drifted helplessly past it. Then she reached a small rock some distance from the island. It was slippery and covered with seaweed, but she clung onto it, her fingers desperately trying to find a hold.

But her body was soaked and numb with the cold, and her hands frozen. The waves crashed over her, and she slipped from the rock back into the swirling sea. Strands of her hair remained entangled in the seaweed, so the rock thereafter became known as Maiden Hair Rock.

The sea was claiming her and her unborn child and so in desperation she prayed to God. The fish which had followed her from Aberlady Bay now began to swim around her, then seals appeared and gulls circled above. She was no longer alone. She scrambled back into her small half-sunk vessel, and now it began to move back into the Firth. Night began to fall and exhaustion overcame her. She closed her eyes, and slipped into unconsciousness.

When the morning mist cleared, a shore appeared before her. There she landed, by Culross in Fife. It was just as well, for there she gave birth to her son, whom she called Kentigern, meaning 'first lord' in her Celtic language.

At that moment some shepherds found her, took pity and warmed her by a fire. They were good men and took news of the maiden with a newly born boy to the local holy man.

He was St Serf who helped raise the child, who became one of the most important saints in Scotland, often called St Mungo, meaning 'my dear friend', patron saint of Glasgow. And so began another great story!

But what of King Loth? His vengeance was now directed towards the swineherd, for he had assumed the poor boy who loved Thenew was to blame for her dishonour. He tried to hunt him down, but the young lad retreated into marshy ground.

And then the hunter became the hunted. The young lad lay in wait for the king close to his fortress home. As Loth passed by, the swineherd threw a spear which pierced and killed him. The legendary King Loth now lay dead in the shadow of his fortress, killed by the man who truly loved his daughter. Tradition says he was buried where he had fallen, and a great stone was erected on the spot as a memorial, forever after known as the Loth Stane.

It is still to be seen, and although its location has been moved slightly, it stands as a memorial to one of East Lothian's great legends.

SCOTTISH BORDERS

JAMES P. SPENCE

JAMES SPENCE is originally from Jedburgh, but now lives in the shadow of Arthur's Seat in Edinburgh. He has had the following books published: Scottish Borders Folk Tales, *graphic novel* Unco Case o Dr Jekyll an Mr Hyde *(Scots version) and three poetry collections. As a storyteller he devised and performed* The Liars Tour *of The Scottish Storytelling Centre. His books* Willow Pattern Haiku, Ghost Paths *[new poems] and* Ferr Frae the Dirlin Thrang *(Scots translation of the Thomas Hardy classic) are expected during 2019.*

THOMAS THE RHYMER

A long time ago on a particularly warm day, Thomas Learmonth frae Ercildoune decided tae go an visit a friend who lived up the Eildon Hills. Hae fancied himself as a bit o a wandering minstrel so hae took his lute with him. It was such a hot day that, having made his way up the slope o Huntlie Bank that lay at the foot o the Eildon Hills, hae decided tae seek the shade o the hawthorn tree there as a place tae sit an rest for a while. After hae got his breath back hae picked up his lute an played a few tunes whilst gazing intae the woods before him. Hae was fascinated by aw the paths that led intae the derkness o the midst o the trees. As hae played hae could hear a trickling sound which hae thought was odd because any spring would surely have dried up because o the long hot summer. But as hae continued tae pluck the strings hae saw a milk-white horse emerging oot o the woods. Aw doon its mane was tied aroond fifty wee bells that jingled like running water. On the back o the horse was a bonnie young lass with long fair hair. She wore a long grass-green silk dress with a derker green velvet mantle on her shoulders. She rode up tae Thomas an hae took the reins an tied them roond a thorny bush. The twae o them sat doon with their backs tae the hawthorn trunk. Though her eyes were as black as coal she was the bonniest lass Thomas had ever seen.

'Thomas, I am the Queen o Elfland an I have come a long way. I would deem it a great favour if ye would play me some tunes, for sweet music an the coolness o the woods go weel together.'

Thomas had tae tear his eyes away frae her canny face as hae took up his lute. An so hae played. His fingers skipped aboot the fretboard mair deftly than they ever had before. After hae had played some half a dozen tunes hae drew tae a finish.

'Thomas, thanks for playing so finely for me. If I can grant ye any favour that's in ma power tae grant, ye only have tae name it.'

Thomas, barefaced as ye like, took her fair hands in his, 'There's only yin thing I want frae ye, ma dear, a kiss frae yer bonnie lips.'

The queen drew back a bit, 'Thomas, if I granted that wish ye do realise I'd have tae take ye back tae Elfland an ye'd be in thrall tae me for seven long years.'

That made nae odds tae Thomas because hae was fair smitten by her loveliness. An so they kissed.

It was the sort o kiss that makes the lips fizz with wonderful possibilities never realised before. It was the sort o kiss that leaves yin full o air an breathless at the same time; the sort o kiss that leaves yin feeling drunk an in need o mair, an yet at the same time mair powerful an alive than ye've ever felt. Such a kiss is like nae other an has been said tae have the merest hint o peppermint aboot its taste, if such an elusive taste can ever be described at aw. Such a kiss has the power tae haunt ye for a lifetime, if ye dinnae watch yersel.

After they'd finished nae other word was said. The Queen o Elfland got up an sclimmed back on tae her horse whilst Thomas untangled the reins frae the bush. The queen left a trailing hand, which Thomas took a hold o an lowped on behind her. The horse set off at a canter through the woods that after a matter o yards led doon hill towards what became kent as the Boglie Burn. When the horse approached the burn, Thomas thought the beast would just lowp across. However, the horse stamped through the middle instead. Some o the water flew oot, catching Thomas in the eyes. Although hae knew this woodland like the back o his hand an though it only took a few seconds tae wipe the water frae his eyes, hae nae longer recognised the woods when hae looked again. Something had subtly altered, the woods were slightly derker, as if the shadows were colluding differently with the light, as if the horse had somehow run intae the reflection o the burn. The horse was picking up pace now an soon it was galloping faster than the four winds, through meadows, glens, hills an woods, an aw the time Thomas could hear the breathing o the far-off ocean thundering in his ears.

Eventually the queen brought the horse tae a stop in a lush green meadow. She sclimmed doon an knelt in the grass. 'Come doon Thomas an rest yer heid in ma lap.'

Thomas fair liked the sound o that an swiftly slid doon off the horse an did as hae was bid. She could toosle his hair an stroke the stubble on his cheeks as much as she liked as far as hae was concerned.

Nae sooner had hae laid his heid on her lap than the horizon started shimmering like a heat-haze for a few moments before clearing again. There appeared three roads before him, replacing the grassy plain that had been there previously. It is said that when ye touch the hem o a seer ye are able tae see through their eyes, seeing anything they can see.

'Ye see that high an rocky road?' the queen asked, 'weel that is the road tae righteousness. For some it is the road tae Heaven, for maist it's the road tae Hell. Ye see that broad straight road in the middle? Weel that is the road tae wickedness, for maist it is the road tae Hell but for a few folk it is the road tae Heaven. Ye see that winding road with a hedge either side? That is the road in-atween, that is the road we're going tae take for it is the road tae Elfland.'

The Queen o Elfland an Thomas got back on the horse's back an set off along that road like the hooves o the very wind. On an on they rode through queer an wondrous landscapes. At times the sky was full o gold-laced cloud, at other times the sky was as black as night. Then they stopped at the edge o a muckle flat grey landscape. A broad red river ran through this bleak place. 'That is aw the blood that humankind has ever shed, an aw the tears they've ever cried. Thomas, if ye ever let on aboot anything ye see or hear in Elfland tae anybody whilst ye're there, ye'll be banished tae this place forever. The fairy folk must never ken ye're human. So ye need tae keep yer mooth shut.'

'I promise ye I'll no say a word.'

They rode on again an finally they saw a pale yellow glow in the distance. Soon after they heard a thousand fairy trumpeters heralding the return o the Queen o Elfland.

Just ootside the gates, Thomas noticed unicorns grazing on the grass below the apple trees.

Now what goes on in Elfland an how Thomas spent his time there nobody rightly kens. Some say it was yin muckle long ceilidh dance the whole time, with endless amounts tae eat an drink o aw description. Others reckon that the fairy folk live on a milky concoction the full time. It is said that Thomas was taken intae seven different rooms tae gie him knowledge an wisdom, the room o colours, the room o mirrors an such like, but little is now kent.

What is generally agreed though is that time passes much quicker in Elfland, so that in hardly a blink in Elfland, folk back in Ercildoune were wondering, what ever happened tae Thomas Learmonth who walked oot yin summer's day twae years ago, an there's been not a trace o him since?

So time passed in Elfland an Thomas served the queen weel, an not a word fell frae his lips tae be caught by those sharp-eared beings. Very soon the seven years had passed, an the queen herself came tae fetch Thomas. She led him oot o the gates o Elfland an the twae were walking through the orchard as unicorns grazed peaceably on the lawns.

'Thomas, I'm grateful tae ye for serving me so loyally these past seven years an no saying a word. Before ye leave I'd like tae gie ye a present.' She reached up an pulled an apple frae an overhanging branch an handed it tae Thomas. 'This is the apple o truth, take it for yerself.'

'I'm no so sure I want it,' said Thomas uncertainly. Thomas was thinking that tae get a decent price for cattle or tae win favour with the lasses ye have tae sometimes exaggerate a bit.

'Thomas, ye'd be wrong tae turn doon this gift. Accept it an ye'll be famous for as long as there is a Scotland, with fine wealth tae match.'

As Thomas dreamed intae her shining eyes, hae found hae could refuse her nothing, so hae slipped the apple intae his jacket pocket.

'Thomas, ye must away now, but I will caw for ye again some day. I'll send twae messengers that ye'll recognise when ye see them.' She then kissed him lightly on the cheek. The scene before him smudged away like a heat-haze. Hae felt his heid spin an the only thing tae hang on tae was the coolness o that kiss.

Hae awoke under the hawthorn tree, with the cauld grass on his cheek in place o the queen's kiss. Lying next tae him was his lute. Hae thought it must have been some fantastic dream till hae rolled ower an felt the lump o the apple in his jacket pocket. Hae got himself up an set off back tae Ercildoune.

As hae walked intae the south o the village a fella saw him an started roaring that Thomas was back frae the deid. Despite seven years passing, Thomas didnae notice a lot o change. The folk that hae kent were a wee bit greyer aboot the temples an parts o his roof needed re-thatching, but that was aboot it. For Thomas life went back tae how it was before. Hae was very popular with the bairns now; they were forever sclimming on tae his knee after mair stories o his ootlandish adventures. As for the apple that hae'd eaten on the way back frae Ercildoune, Thomas never noticed any difference tae the way hae went aboot his business. It seemed that truth was having nae effect, at least not at first.

There came a time when the folk in the village had a meeting, for they were very worried aboot the fact that there were a lot o cattle dying roond aboot. As the meeting went on folk were getting mair an mair agitated, until in the thick o the row, Thomas lowped tae his feet, as if his body were nae longer his ain, an his mooth said that not yin coo would die within Ercildoune. Hae had spoken in such a calm steady voice that everyone heeded him. An so it came tae pass that not yin coo perished.

After that Thomas got himself a reputation, an before very long folk frae aw ower came tae get advice on aw sorts o things, frae what crops tae plant, the weather, an suitable young men an suitable young women for prospective marriage partners. Soon hae was famous far an wide with money tae match, because lairds an the like would value his wisdom an his insight. Hae became kent as Thomas the Rhymer, or True Thomas. Hae made many prophesies, an they always came oot in rhyme. Many o which, in the fullness o time, turned oot tae be true.

Hae prophesied that there would come a time when Scotland would be cut in twae. An folk thought how could such a thing be possible, but it came tae pass when the Caledonian Canal was built, stretching frae Loch Ness tae Crinan in the west.

With Thomas' growing wealth hae built himself a muckle hoose cawed Rhymer's Tower at the south end o Ercildoune. Every year hae would have the grandest celebration there. Everybody would be invited, rich an poor alike. This particular year the dancers had just finished dancing an Thomas was playing a few tunes on his lute when a servant charged in saying there was the strangest sight oot on the road. For there was a milk-white hart an a milk-white hind just standing there, tame as ye like. Everybody made their way oot with Thomas at the heid o them. Everyone just stood as if in a dream as Thomas sauntered ower tae the twae deer. Then Thomas an the twae deer aboot turned an sauntered away frae Ercildoune. Thomas the Rhymer was never seen again. Hae'd gone back tae Elfland tae be with his queen again.

❖

NOTE – ye can still see the ruins o Rhymer's Tower tae this very day, behind the petrol garage at the south end o Earlston, formerly Ercildoune.

THE LADDIE THAT KEPT HARES

At the side o the Happertutie Burn, that trickles intae the Yarrow before it flows intae St Mary's Loch, there was a tumble-doon cottage, where a poor widow-woman an her twae strapping sons lived. There wasnae much work tae be had at that time, an even less tae eat, so there came a time when the eldest son announced that hae was going tae go oot intae the world tae earn his fortune.

On hearing this his mother said, 'Aye, weel, whatever will be will be,' an handed him a sieve an a cracked bowl frae the kitchen table. 'Away tae the well for some water. The mair water ye bring back the bigger the bannock I'll bake for yer journey.'

Just by the Happertutie Burn there's a steep slope where the well was. Next tae the well was a briar bush amongst the rushes. But what the laddie didnae notice was a bonnie wee bird in the bush singing tae the blue sky up yonder. The minute the wee bird saw the laddie with the sieve an the bowl hae changed his song.

Stop it with fog, an clag it with clay,
and that'll carry the water away.

'Away ye go ye stupid wee birdie. Do ye think I'm going tae dirty ma hands just because ye tell me tae?'

The bird flew away. O course the water just run oot o the sieve every time the laddie pulled the sieve oot o the well, an the cracked bowl wasnae very much better, an so the laddie hurried back tae his mother as fast as hae could with only drips on the mesh o the sieve an only a wee drop o water in the bowl. On seeing such a wee drop o water the widow-woman just sighed, an was only able tae make him a wee bannock with oatmeal.

When the bannock had cooled the laddie was in such a rush tae get going hae didnae hang aroond for his mother's blessing an neither did hae even say cheerio tae his brother.

Hae strode through the birch trees an ower the Yarrow Hills. When hae got tired hae stopped under a birch tree on the side o a hill tae rest. Hae then pulled oot the wee bannock, an was just aboot tae take a bite oot o it when a wee bird fluttered doon an landed on a branch beside him.

'Gie me a bite o yer bannock an I'll gie ye yin o ma wing-feathers so ye can make yersel a pair o pipes.'

'Ye stupid wee birdie, what do I want with a pair o pipes when I'm off tae find ma fortune. It's yer silly fault I've got such a tottie-wee bannock. There's hardly enough for me, let alone waste it on the likes o ye. Howts, away with ye an take yer bad luck with ye.' The bird flew off an the laddie ate his bannock.

On hae walked through birches an ower the hills o Yarrow, until by an by hae came tae a hoose where a king happened tae live.

'This will do me,' said the laddie tae himself, an in hae walked an asked if there was any work for a strapping lad such as himself.

'What can ye do?' asked the king.

'Oh, I can look after the coos, take oot the ashes an sweep the floor.'

'I see,' said the king, 'and do ye think ye could look after hares?'

The laddie considered this, an thought that if hae could look after sheep an cattle hae could surely look after hares.

'Aye, I can look after hares.'

'Grand,' said the king rubbing his hands together, 'tomorrow ye'll have ma hares tae look after. If ye bring them back safe an sound at night ye'll get tae marry ma daughter.'

'Suits me just fine,' said the laddie, thinking how easy it was going tae be tae earn his fortune an marry a princess intae the bargain.

'But if ye dinnae bring them back safely I'll hang ye by the neck the very next day.'

The laddie didnae like the sound o this, but hae'd given his word tae the king so hae couldnae very weel go back on it now. The king didnae mention anything aboot supper but instead showed the laddie tae his room. Hae slept as sound as could be.

The laddie woke early the next morning an jumped intae his claes an made his way quickly doon the stairs in the hope o being given some breakfast. Alas the king had already finished off aw the breakfast that there had been, the porridge, the bannocks an aw o the ale. Aw the laddie was offered was a mere cup o water.

'When ye've drunk that I want ye tae get away doon tae the Auld Dyke Field where ma hares are playing. Look after them for me an bring them back safe at night an put them in the barn.'

So off went the laddie, grumbling tae himself as hae went, 'What a way tae treat a laddie that's going tae marry a princess. I mean I only had a tottie-wee bannock tae eat on ma travels yesterday, an not a morsel this morning.'

When the laddie got tae the Auld Dyke Field hae saw the hares playing in the long grass. Hae counted twenty-four hares, an then hae noticed another hare, a wee yin with a hoppilly leg. Hae chased after the hares, an they immediately scattered, aw except the wee yin with the hoppilly leg, which hae quickly caught by the lugs. Hae skinned it an roasted it ower a fire. Then after eating the wee hare hae fell fast asleep an didnae waken till many hours later tae immediately see that the sun had gone doon tae just above the trees.

The laddie quickly roused himself an chased after the hares, but the hares scattered even faster than before, having seen what hae done tae the wee hare with the hoppilly leg.

Sometime later hae arrived wearily back at the king's hoose. The king immediately asked o him, 'Did ye look after ma hares?'

'Aye, I looked after yer hares.'

'And did ye bring them back an put them in ma barn?'

'Naw, I wasnae able tae bring them back …'

So that was the laddie hanged by the neck the very next morning.

A year after the laddie had left the wee cottage next tae the Happertutie Burn his younger brother approached his mother an said tae her that it was aboot time hae went oot intae the world tae earn his fortune.

On hearing this his mother said, 'Aye, weel, whatever will be will be,' an handed him a sieve an a cracked bowl frae the kitchen table. 'Away tae the well for some water. The mair water ye bring back the bigger the bannock I'll bake for yer journey.'

So the laddie took the bowl an the sieve an went doon tae the well by the Happertutie Burn. Next tae the well, amongst the rushes, was a briar bush an in it was a bonnie wee bird singing tae the blue sky up yonder. The minute the wee bird saw the laddie with the sieve an the bowl hae changed his song.

Stop it with fog, an clag it with clay,
and that'll carry the water away.

'Hey ma bonnie wee birdie, thank ye very much,' the laddie said, an set aboot lining the sieve with moss frae the side o the burn, an filling in the cracks o the bowl with clay frae under the banking o the burn. Then hae filled them both with water frae the well an carefully carried them hame.

On seeing the amount o water her laddie had managed tae collect his mother was fair toorled an baked a grand big bannock with aw o the water an oatmeal.

Yince the bannock had cooled the laddie said tae his mother, 'I'd fair like yer blessing along with the bannock.' His mother sighed an smiled an gave him a big cuddle before watching him go.

Hae strode through the birch trees an ower the Yarrow Hills. When hae got tired hae stopped on the side o a hill under a birch tree tae rest. Hae then pulled oot the bannock, broke it in twae an put yin half back in his bag. Hae was just aboot tae take a bite oot o the bannock when the wee bird fluttered doon an landed on a branch beside him.

'Gie me a bite o yer bannock an I'll gie ye yin o ma wing-feathers so ye can make yersel a pair o pipes.'

'Ye're welcome tae eat yer fill ma bonnie wee bird, cos it was you that told me how tae fog the sieve with moss an clag the bowl with clay so that I could carry aw that water back tae ma mother.' Hae broke off a bit for the bird, then halved what was left, put yin half in his pocket an ate what was left.

After the bird had pecked up every crumb the wee birdie said, 'That was braw. Now, if ye will pull a feather oot o ma wing ye can make yersel a pair o pipes.'

'Ach, I couldnae do such a thing tae ye. I wouldnae want tae hurt ye.'

'Naw, naw, it'll nae hurt me a bit. Just do what I tell ye. Now here, take yin o ma wing-feathers, an make yersel a pair o pipes.'

Not wishing tae offend the bonnie wee bird, the laddie started tae pull at yin o the wing-feathers. Hae was amazed that it came away so easily. The laddie then watched how the bonnie wee bird fluttered off intae the braw blue sky an was soon lost in the sun.

By an by hae took oot his knife, an carefully cut the barbs off the feather. Then hae cut the shaft in half an notched them both. When hae had fashioned the pipes hae put them tae his lips, an the tune that came oot as hae played was the same song as the bonnie wee bird had sung tae the blue sky up yonder.

Now instead o walking, hae danced tae the magical tune o his pipes as hae made his way through the birches an ower the hills o Yarrow until, at the hinderend, hae arrived at the hoose where the king lived.

'Maybe this is the place I'll earn ma fortune,' said the laddie tae himself, as hae knocked on the door. Moments later the king himself answered the door.

'I'm oot in the world tae earn ma fortune, so I wondered if ye had anything needing doing yer highness.'

'What can ye do?' asked the king.

'Oh, I can look after the coos, take oot the ashes an sweep the floor.'

'I see,' said the king, 'and do ye think ye could look after hares?'

The younger brother considered this, an thought that if hae could look after sheep an cattle, seeing tae it that they didnae stray, hae could surely look after hares.

'Aye, I can look after hares.'

'Grand,' said the king rubbing his hands together, 'tomorrow ye'll have ma hares tae look after. If ye bring them back safe an sound at night ye'll get tae marry ma daughter.'

'That suits me just fine,' said the laddie, 'as long as it suits yer daughter.'

'Ye just look tae yer ain sel an let me think aboot ma daughter,' said the king brusquely. 'And mind, if ye dinnae bring aw ma hares back safely I'll hang ye by the neck the very next morning.'

The laddie didnae like the sound o this, but hae'd given his word tae the king so hae couldnae very weel back oot o it now. The king didnae mention anything aboot supper but showed the laddie straight tae his room instead. Hae took what was left o the bannock, broke it in twae, an after eating yin bit hae fell fast asleep.

Hae woke early the next morning an jumped intae his claes, making his way quickly doon the stairs just in time tae see that the king had already finished off aw the breakfast that there had been, the porridge, the bannocks an aw o the ale. Aw the laddie was offered was a mere cup o water.

'When ye've drunk that I want ye tae get away doon tae the Auld Dyke Field where ma hares are playing. Look after them for me an bring them back safe the night. Oh an mind tae put them in the barn.'

Away went the laddie tae the Auld Dyke Field. When hae arrived hae counted twenty-four hares playing in the long grass. Then hae noticed a wee hare with a hoppilly leg. As hae watched them hae took oot the remainder o his bannock an hae ate every last crumb o it.

Then, wondering how hae might pass the time, hae pulled oot his pipes an started tae play. Hae played that bonnie that the hares stopped their games an just looked at him. Then they started tae dance, coming closer an closer tae him as they did so, until they formed a circle aroond him. An the air was filled with ever so bonnie pipe music.

Aw aroond an everywhere there was a magic stillness. The fish snoozled in the stream, water birds snoozled in the reeds, aw the critters o the fields snoozled in the shade. Aw was still an aw snoozled forby the hares at the playing o the pipes.

Aw day long the hares danced. It was only when the laddie saw the sun poised ower the trees in the west that hae stopped his playing. Only then did the hares stop their dancing. Only then did aw the other creatures stir frae their glamour.

'Now we must away hame,' said the laddie, putting his pipes in his pocket. Hae wondered how hae might get the hares tae go with him. Hae got up anyway an took a few steps, an found that the hares were following him. But then hae saw the wee hare with the hoppilly leg. Hae felt sorry for it an so lifted it up an put it inside his jacket tae keep it warm. As hae patted its heid an stroked its lugs hae gazed intae its muckle broon eyes, an couldnae help thinking that they were the maist beautiful eyes hae had ever seen. The laddie walked on an the twenty-four hares seemed very happy tae follow him given that hae was looking after the wee hare with the hoppilly leg.

When hae arrived back at the hoose the king asked him, 'Weel, did ye look after ma hares?'

'Aye, I did that.'

'An did ye bring them back an put them in the barn?'

'Aye, I did.'

'Away an fetch them for me.'

The laddie duly brought the twenty-four hares tae the king.

'That's fine, fine, but what did ye do with the other hare?'

'I took the wee yin with the hoppilly leg up the stairs an put her in ma bed tae keep her warm.'

'Away an fetch her for me.'

The laddie went up the stairs tae his room, but there was nae hare in his bed at aw. For in its place was a lassie with long shiny hair an the maist bonnie broon eyes hae'd seen in aw his days. Hae brought the lassie doon the stairs tae the king.

'Weel laddie, it seems as if ye've lost a hare an found a princess,' said the king, fair toorled. 'Ye'll be married the morn.'

'That's fine by me, as long as it's fine by yer daughter.'

The princess said that she thought she might like the laddie, but needed a wee bit o time tae think aboot it.

'Maybe ye would like a wee bit o music whilst ye're thinking?' put in the laddie.

The king glowered at him. The laddie had nae idea that the king hated music, but it was too late, hae already had the pipes up tae his mooth, an the hoose was soon reverberating with the magical tune hae'd learnt frae the bonnie wee birdie. Aw at yince aw o the servants stopped seeing tae their chores an set aboot dancing, along with the twenty-four hares an the princess an even the auld king himself. An they danced aw night till the sun rose yince again. By now the princess had decided that she did have a liking for the laddie, an that she would marry him.

'Weel,' said the king fair pleased, 'now that that's sorted oot, let's get this wedding on the go.'

'What, now?' asked the laddie.

'Weel, there's nae reason tae tarry,' said the king, 'now is there?'

'It's just that I'd like ma mother tae be there. She bides in a tumble-doon cottage at the side o the Happertutie Burn!'

When the laddie's mother was sent for the king immediately gave her a wee cottage tae live in near tae his ain hoose. As for the laddie an the princess they had the grandest wedding, with guests frae aw ower Ettrick, the Tweed an Yarrow. Years after when the auld king passed away, the laddie that had looked after the hares ruled in his place.

⁂

NOTE – Although this story took place a very long time ago, that cottage at the side o the Happertutie Burn is still there tae this very day. Nae doot it is in a better state o repair than it was back then.

DUMFRIES & GALLOWAY

TONY BONNING

TONY BONNING is a full-time author, poet, musician and storyteller with twenty books published and sales of over a million copies. He is constantly on tour, doing up to 300 shows a year (usually two a day). He is founder of the annual Galloway Children's Festival, the Young Bands Project for teenagers and the weekly Play it by Ear pre-school music group. Born on the edge of the mountains of south-west Scotland, Tony's inspirations are his wife, the land, the people and the language of his forebears.

THE MILK WHITE DOO

Jacob and Wilhelm Grimm collected märchen or folk tales in their native Germany. Their collection is certainly the best known in the world of folk tales. When translated into English, what became apparent to other collectors such as James Halliwell, J.F. Campbell, William Chambers and others was the commonality of many of the tales. No doubt storytellers took tales from books, such as Grimms', that they then used, but more usually the tales were oral and travelled along the highways and seaways of the world every which way: Cinderella probably started in China, hence the shoe only fitting one specific foot, and versions of the famed Brer Rabbit can be found in Africa and China. The following tale would seem to have a common source with the Grimms' 'Juniper Tree', because of the close similarity of the repetitive refrain. But, as in most tales, it takes on something of the culture where it is told. Similar versions are found in Hungary, Romania, Austria and England, and this one is from Scotland. Be warned, it is a shocking tale for adults. Unsurprisingly – to storytellers – it is very popular with children.

❖

Long ago there was a man called Alan Hunter who fell in love with a girl called Belle. Though not the brightest of souls, Alan was loving and kind and relentlessly courted Belle for a year and a day. In the end, she agreed to marry him. The marriage was blissful and they worked together on their little croft on the long plain, *Am Magh Fada* in Gaelic, which gives the town of Moffat its name. Because of their hard work they prospered and so leased more land until they had a substantial farm and moorland for summer grazing. They had a small herd of sheep, six milk cows and numerous chickens, ducks and geese. They also had ten acres of arable land which they formed into rigs, or ridges – unfenced raised strips of soil, for growing oats, barley, hay and flax for clothing. On the in-by fields near the farm they built dykes to safeguard the animals and to keep them away from their crops in the out-by fields.

They had been five years married when winter came early. The land was dusted with snow, yet there were still leaves on the rowan tree that stood to the side, or cheek, of their front door. The young woman looked at the tree and made a wish that she would have a child with hair red like the rowan and skin as fair as the new snow. Soon after, the young woman found she was pregnant, and on a warm day in August she gave birth to a baby boy whom she named Johnnie. He had a shock of thick red hair and his skin seemed to shine white with an inner light. However, the birth was difficult, complications arose and, with no skilled surgeon within fifty miles, she died. Family gathered round and gave Alan support in his grief and a wet nurse was found for the child. In time, Alan settled down to life as a single parent. To remind him of the purity and beauty of his wife, he set two large white quartz stones beneath the rowan tree.

Running the farm on his own was hard and he thought it best and practical to get some extra help. He hired a young, unemployed man called Hugh Bowman who brought along his sister Morag to help in the house. The girl's common-law husband had deserted her, and with a young daughter to care for was glad of the work. While Hugh was an adequate worker, his sister, also not the brightest of souls, was excellent. Morag had a hard edge, and when it came to chopping a chicken for the pot or taking a knife to the throat of a braxy sheep at the back end of the year, she did so without a second thought. What Alan especially liked was that her daughter Katie had great maternal instincts and spent her time playing with Johnnie, who had just started to crawl. She insisted on feeding, washing and generally caring for the boy.

A month later, Hugh was offered a job at a neighbouring farm with a higher wage. Though sad to see him go, Alan was quite happy he did not have to pay out two wages and his own; he could manage with Morag's help. Shortly after, it seemed right and decent to Alan that, if Morag was living under the same roof, perhaps they should be properly married. Morag seemed happy enough with the arrangement, no doubt feeling more secure about Katie's and her future. By this time, Alan loved Katie as if she were his own daughter and was fond of Morag, even with her occasional highly strung emotions. They had a penny wedding where neighbours and friends contributed a penny each to the celebrations. They settled down to family life, and though Morag was occasionally hard on Johnnie, this was mitigated by the obvious affection Katie had for the lad. She also insisted that he should not be called her 'stepbrother' but simply her 'brother'.

In the first year of their marriage things went well in the home and on the farm. There was a good harvest and the children especially enjoyed the trip to the mill in Moffat to grind the corn. They paid the miller in meal then took a bag – the melder – to poor people in the village. Alan also visited the local silversmith and had a bracelet made for Morag – he missed the look of disappointment in

Katie's eyes as they passed the dress shop that she had not got something, though he did buy liquorice to make sugarallie water:

Sugarallie *water,*   lichorice
as black as the lum,   chimney
If ye gether up yer preens,   pins
I'll gie *ye some.*   give

They sang as they poured hot water over the black sticks.

The second year of their marriage was hard. It had been especially rainy and the crops had not thrived. The animals suffered in the wet pasture and grew less healthy, and some died. Milk production dropped and Alan was loathed to shear the sheep in the continuing cold. Taking the sheep on to the hill was misery but he had to herd them against theft. His oilskins kept out the worst of the rain but he could never sit for any length of time as he would grow cold. While his dogs never complained, they looked quite miserable. Back on the farm, the children kept a watchful eye on the cattle when they were out-by to stop them straying into the meagre crops. Morag kept house, did spinning and sowing and looking after the poultry, though even their egg production had dwindled; only the ducks and geese seemed impervious to the wet. Although not on the point of starvation, other people were, and things were worrying, for animals were disappearing from neighbouring farms. Alan decided that he would take his musket with him next time he took the sheep to the hill. For a change, the evening was dry and pleasant and the sun setting to the north-north-west sank into a bed of fire. The night would be light, but it was time he was home to see the children before bed. He had only gone twenty yards when a hare rose in front of him. On impulse, he raised the musket and fired. It was a clean shot and the animal dropped instantly. At the same time the sheep fled the bang, as did the sheepdogs. It was late before he had gathered them up and herded them back to the farm. Morag was piqued at the late arrival and the children were already asleep. He dropped the hare on the table and explained what had occurred.

She replied, 'Huv ye nae brain? Ye micht hae kennt the blast wid send them fleein.'

Because of tiredness and having been teased mercilessly about his brawn and no brain as a child, Alan fumed, 'Caain the kettle black? Ye hae little wit yersel!'

With the stress of present circumstances, both exploded into fury and railed at each other, waking the children in the process. The howls and tears of the children quietened the feuding pair. That night Alan slept on the rug by the fire. First thing in the morning he was away to the hill with the sheep.

When Morag rose from her sleep, darkness had crept into her soul; deep resentments murmured along the boundaries of her mind; confusion and madness skirmished in her thoughts. As if in a trance, she saw to the children's breakfast then sent them to let out the poultry and collect any eggs while she milked the cows, slapping at them furiously if they moved. While the children took the cows to the out-by pasture, Morag strained the milk, put in the churn then went back into the house to prepare the hare. With manic relish she gutted and skinned the carcase and placed it in the cauldron. Wielding the kitchen knife like a weapon of war she chopped onions, carrots and parsnips, dropped them into the pot and added some water. She set it to hang just above the fire to slow-cook. After an hour she added more peats and stirred the stew. Two hours later, as she added more peats, she couldn't resist a taste of the flesh. It was delicious. She found herself returning again and again to the stew until there were only vegetables left. Manically she paced the room, knife in hand, muttering threats and fears about Alan: 'I should poison the damned stew. But he'll go for me again; might even beat me if there's no hare in the pot.' Just then, Johnnie toddled through the door; his innocent face looked up at his step-mother. In that moment Morag's mind snapped. She lifted Johnnie by the arm, placed him on the table and chopped his head off. She dismembered the body, dropped it all into the cauldron and brought it to the boil with some brushwood. The stew was then gently simmered for the rest of the day. As it cooked, Morag threw herself down on the bed and fell asleep.

Katie, who was sitting on a rock looking after the cows, watched Johnnie as he padded off towards the farm. As he went round a building out of sight she kept an eye out for his return. He was gone too long so she decided to run back to the farm to get him – the cows were hobbled so it was safe to leave them for five minutes. She first checked the outbuildings then, not finding him, went to the house. The door was open and she could see her mother asleep on the bed. She looked in the door but could not see Johnnie. The sweet smell of cooking was overpowering so she went over to the cauldron and peeped in. Looking back at her was the face of her brother. She reeled back gasping in horror. The sound woke Morag who sat up and rubbed her eyes. Katie looked at her mother with shock and fear. Morag rose from the bed with a look of fury. She took two steps across the floor and grabbed Katie by the hair. She leaned forward to within a few inches of Katie's face.

'If ye say a word o this tae yer faither ye will end up in the pot yersel. Dae ye unnerstaun?'

Her face white with terror and her eyes brimming with tears of fear and loss, Katie could barely nod.

Her mother threw her to the floor. 'Get oot o ma sicht an see tae they coos.'

The lass ran from the house towards the meadow, howling in distress. She had watched her mother over the years and could never understand why sometimes she would seem caring then other times she would become like a demon, though rarely in front of Alan. It was the children who suffered most.

Katie stayed away all day, too much in terror of what might happen when she returned. She delayed as late as possible until the cows became agitated and began hobbling towards the farm. She undid the hobbles and the cows sprinted off towards the byre. They arrived at the same time as Alan and the sheep from the hill, which were driven in beside the cows for security. Katie arrived just as Alan was chaining and padlocking the door. He stepped forward, put his hands under her armpits, lifted her and planted a kiss on her cheeks.

'Hoo are ye, ma bonnie wee lass?' Although she felt safer now he was home, she dreaded what was to come and could not look him in the face. Instead she laid her head on his shoulder and snuggled in. She felt his powerful hand gently stroke her hair as they went in the house.

Although the atmosphere inside was tense, Alan, while setting Katie down, attempted to ease things.

'My, that's a grand smell. What is it?' he said amiably.

'It's the hare that ye shot,' Morag said abruptly, throwing a threatening look at Katie.

'Disnae smell like hare,' he replied innocently.

'That's because I pit ither things in the pot as weel,' she said sarcastically.

'Aye, of course.'

Alan went to the sideboard and carried over four wooden bowls and four horn spoons.

'Jist set it fer twa,' said Morag, 'I'm no hungry and the boy's sleepin.'

Alan set two places and put two bowls and spoons back on the sideboard.

'I'm no hungersome either,' said Katie, before sloping off to bed in tears.

'Whit's up wi the weans?' asked Alan.

'Nae idea,' said Morag, Picking up Alan's bowl and walking over to the cauldron. She ladled the stew into the bowl and set it before Alan. He supped a spoonful of juice before lifting some onion.

Through the curtain of the inset bed, Katie looked on in horror as she saw him lift a spoonful of flesh. It slipped off the spoon and fell back in the bowl. Katie willed him not to pick it up again. Instead of using his spoon, he picked it up with his fingers.

'Would ye luik at that,' he said, with a laugh. 'It luiks jist like wee Johnnie's haun.'

Katie gasped and threw herself face down on the heather-flower pillow.

'Yer haiverin,' said Morag. 'It wis a muckle hare.'

Alan ate the limb and set about the rest with relish. Halfway through he picked up another piece of flesh, gave a laugh and said, 'That's like wee Johnnie's fit.'

Katie pressed the pillow into her ears so as not to hear any more.

'Wid ye haud yer wheesht an jist eat yer meat,' said Morag sharply. Alan made a face of resignation and finished his meal. After he had finished, Morag blew out the candles.

'Bedtime,' she said, expecting no protest.

Katie lay awake and heard her mother and father fall asleep. There was still some light in the sky from the summer sun and a full moon. With the silence of a cat, she climbed from the bed and made her way to the cauldron. She eased it off the pot hook and carried it to the door. As she lifted the sneck, the click caused Alan to stir. Katie stood in silence until he had settled then slid open the door and stepped outside, pulling the door towards her without closing it. She went to the toolstore to get a bucket. With the bucket in one hand and the cauldron in the other, she walked down to the burn. There under the light of a ghost moon she quietly and reverently removed Johnnie's bones from the cauldron, washed each one in the clear water and placed them in the bucket. Katie then walked back to the door of the house, set down the cauldron and bucket and lifted the quartz stones. Using a flat stone, she dug out the soil and then placed Johnnie's bones in the hole. Next she covered them with the quartz. Using the flat stone she scattered the spare soil from the hole, careful to tread it flat with her feet. After replacing the bucket in the toolstore she went back to the quartz stone, kneeled down and kissed it. She then kissed the rowan tree, gathered up the cauldron and crept back into the house. The cauldron went back on the hook and then Katie slipped into bed. She lay for ages thinking about her beloved brother and his gruesome fate as hot tears dripped on to the pillow; gradually sleep overtook her.

As dawn paled the eastern sky the rowan began to quiver and a small shower of leaves floated down on to the quartz. As for the bones that lay beneath:

They grew, and they grew,
Tae a milk-white doo,   dove
That tuik tae *its wings,*   took to
An awa *it flew.*   away

The bird flew off in the direction of Moffat. When it came to the River Annan it turned north until it came to a group of women gossiping at the shallows as they washed new garments to make ready to sell. The dove alighted on an alder tree and began to coo:

Pew, pew, ma mammy me slew,
Pew, pew, ma daddy me chew,
Ma dear sister Katie she getherit ma banes, gathered my bones
An set them ablow *twa milk-white stanes;*   below
Whaur I grew, and grew tae a milk-white doo,
Then I tuik to my wings, and awa I flew.

Fascinated by the dove's refrain, one cried out:

Wee doo, wee doo, oh bonnie wee doo
Wid ye sing yer wee sang again fer us noo?

The dove cocked its head to side and said:

Aye, if ye wull cease yer clashin   gossip
An gie me aa the claes ye're washin.

They all looked at each other and nodded, so the dove repeated the refrain,

Pew, pew, ma mammy me slew,
Pew, pew, ma daddy me chew,
Ma dear sister Katie she getherit ma banes,
An set them ablow twa milk-white stanes;
Whaur I grew, and grew tae a milk-white doo,
Then I tuik to my wings, and awa I flew.

The women laid aside the garments and the dove flew down and, with unearthly strength, lifted the clothes in its claws and flew on towards Moffat. It set the clothes down on a roof and flew on to the window ledge of the silver-smith. The smith was just sitting down at his workbench and had laid out a pile of silver coins that he was about to melt down and turn into jewellery when the dove began to call:

Pew, pew, ma mammy me slew,
Pew, pew, ma daddy me chew,
Ma dear sister Katie she getherit ma banes,
An set them ablow twa milk-white stanes;
Whaur I grew, and grew tae a milk-white doo,
Then I tuik to my wings, and awa I flew.

The jeweller turned and stared in fascination at the bird on his window sill.

My, whit an antrin *sang ye sing.*   strange
Wull ye sing it again, ma bonnie wee thing?

Hopping on to the window frame, the dove said:

I wull sing the sang fer ye
If aa yer siller *coins ye'll gie.*   silver

The smith nodded his head and laid the coins on the window sill, and the milk-white dove sang his song:

Pew, pew, ma mammy me slew,
Pew, pew, ma daddy me chew,
Ma dear sister Katie she getherit ma banes,
An set them ablow twa milk-white stanes;
Whaur I grew, and grew tae a milk-white doo,
Then I tuik to my wings, and awa I flew.

With claws and beak he gathered up the coins and flew on to the roof. Wrapping the coins in the clothes he flew to the mill. Leaving the clothes and coins on the roof, the dove flew down and through the mill door. The miller had opened the millrace and set the millwheel turning. He engaged the grinding stones and turned to get a bag of meal sitting against a spare millstone. The dove settled on a beam above the miller's head and began to call out:

Pew, pew, ma mammy me slew,
Pew, pew, ma daddy me chew,
Ma dear sister Katie she getherit ma banes,
An set them ablow twa milk-white stanes;
Whaur I grew, and grew tae a milk-white doo,
Then I tuik to my wings, and awa I flew.

Even over the sound of the turning stones, the plaintive call could be clearly heard. The miller disconnected the gear and turned to the dove:

Hoch! Hoch! Ma bonnie wee doo
Will ye sing for me again een nou?   even (right) now

The bird fluttered down on to the spare millstone:

I will sing ma sang again
If ye will gie me this mill stane.

The miller nodded his head, agreeing to the bargain.

Pew, pew, ma mammy me slew,
Pew, pew, ma daddy me chew,
Ma dear sister Katie she getherit ma banes,
An set them ablow twa milk-white stanes;
Whaur I grew, and grew tae a milk-white doo,
Then I tuik to my wings, and awa I flew.

The dove now grabbed the great millstone in its claws and, to the astonishment of the miller, lifted it into the air and flew out through the open door. Hovering in the air beside the roof, the dove took up the clothes and coins in its beak and flew southwards back towards the farm. Further down the river was an old dead tree. The dove hovered by it, leaning the great stone against its trunk. The clothes with the coins it hung among the dried-out branches, then perched on a twig and waited.

As the sun set it flew on to the farm, gliding in after Alan had come home. It gently laid the millstone against the back of the house and dropped the clothes and coins on the thatch of the roof. It then flew to the ground and gathered up small stones in its beak; these it dropped down the chimney.

Inside Katie lay on the bed in a state of misery. She heard the sound from the fireplace as the pebbles fell into or bounced off the cauldron. Somehow she knew it was a message and ran for the door. Outside, she automatically looked up to see beautiful new clothes floating down towards her. With joy she reached up and caught them.

In the same instant Alan came through the door, curious at Katie's behaviour, in time to see Katie reach up for the falling garments. He looked up to see where they had come from and as he did so ten silver coins flashed past his head and bounced on the ground at his feet. With a laugh, he picked them up then looked again to the sky but nothing was there. In puzzlement, he looked at Katie's smiling face.

On seeing her daughter's strange behaviour and hearing Alan's laugh, Morag walked out the door to see what was happening. Outside, both Katie and Alan were looking in amazement towards the sky. She looked up but only had a brief moment to see the great mass of the millstone falling towards her. The impact was so great that the monolith sank right up to its rim in the ground.

So fast had things happened that Alan and Katie had not seen Morag emerge from the house and so, caught up in the sight of the dove as it hovered like an angel above them, they did not see the fatal act. It was the sound of the impact that turned their heads in shock. They looked up again to the dove as it hovered in the soft blue light of the evening sky. With a soft coo it began to ascend higher and higher. They followed its now glittering whiteness as it soared upwards until it disappeared into the heavens.

Through sobs, Katie told all that had happened the day before. Alan was stricken with guilt and horrified at the idea that he had eaten the flesh of his own son; but Katie said that the dove was the departing spirit of Johnnie and the coins were proof that he must not feel such things. She proved the point by lifting the quartz stones; there was nothing beneath them except three milk-white feathers.

Alan raised Katie as his own, and in time she married an honest young man from Moffat. A year later they had a son and named him Johnnie.

THE PUDDOCK

A young man's father died and left him his small estate. The new laird, whose name was Alexander – Sandy to his friends – decided he would be the man that his father was. His father had been autocratic, arrogant and something of a bully to those around him; especially to women, whom he thought of as second-class citizens. His mother, a good and kind woman, had died of consumption when Alexander was just a boy. Alexander had something of her about him but felt that his father's way must be the right way – his father had told him as much.

Many of the workers on the estate were glad to see the back of the old laird and hoped for better from Alexander. They were to be disappointed. Alexander wanted to prove he was all the man his father was. However, the old laird was naturally mean; Alexander had to work at it and consequently was even more bumptious. He devised new plans for the estate and when his factor protested that it was unviable, he sacked the man. Later he threw an old couple out of their cottage as he deemed them too old to be of use any more. He closed the estate school – his father's one act of decency – for being a drain on his finances. As the estate faltered he blamed everyone but himself, much in the manner his father had done before him. Like the old laird, he treated everyone with disdain and most especially women. When with his friends he would try to outdo them in all things, especially chasing young women, and gained a reputation as a Romeo. In his quiet hours he would chastise himself for his meanness; he would then hear his father's voice rebuking him as being weak. He spent many a night in torment.

It was a cold, sleety day when Meg o the Moor came down from the hills above Moniaive to spend the cold season by the coast. Her winter home was in a half-thatched former cot house on the edge of the estate. She lived off shellfish and the kindness of local people. In return, she cured many an illness with her knowledge of herbs and roots. She had been tolerated by the old laird for she had once eased his gout with apple vinegar and cherries. Alexander had no gout and when he found out she was living on his land rent-free he went to evict her.

He rode up to the semi-derelict cottage and shouted on her, 'Are ye in there Meg? Come oot!'

The old woman came to the ramshackle door and leaned on her stick. 'It's yersel, young Sandy. Whit can I dae fer ye. Are ye ill, young sir?'

'Indeed, I am no ill and I dinnae need yer cantrips. Whit I need is for you tae vacate this hoose eenou. That is unless ye are prepared to pey a bawbee fer each week ye stey here.'

Meg looked at the young man calmly and said, 'Ye ken yer faither said I cuid stey here as lang as I liked; an fer nae kane either.'

'Aye well, he's deid. Noo be aff wi ye. That is unless ye hae the kane.'

'Ye are an arrogant young man an deservin o a lesson in guid manners.'

In a fury Alexander raised his whip. He did not intend to hit Meg but rather to frighten her. With an unexpected speed she raised her stick and his arm froze in mid-air. His eyes widened in horror, so sure was he that he was about to be spellbound and subjected to the horrors of Hell.

'Ye hae something o yer faither aboot ye, young Sandy; but I sense that deep in yer hert is the guidness o yer mither.

I think ye need a wee bittie time tae fellthocht that.' She stepped up to the catatonic Alexander and touched his waist with her stick. He instantly turned into a frog. Meg reached up to the saddle and lifted him down and dropped him into the pocket of her pinafore. She then went inside and gathered up her bonnet and cloak and set out on a journey.

As she walked she talked. 'We womenfolk hae lang hud tae pit up wi menfolk thinkin they are somethin special; aye, an there's mibbe a few womenfolk that think the same. But ye see, Sandy, yer mither cairryit ye inside her belly and grew ye intae a fine strong lad; she sufferit unimaiginable pain tae bring ye intae the warld; she nursit ye frae her ain breist an she wipit yer erse foreby. Noo is that no worthy o respect? I ken weel that the fate o a man is hard tae, oot there tryin tae provide fer their faimily. But the wifie is no exactly relaxin at hame wi her seiven weans and a supper tae pit on the table; aye, an whiles oot workin in the fields aside their men as weel.'

Meg was now in her stride, both physically and mentally. Her talk was as brisk as her walk. 'An talkin aboot these men and women that wark fer ye i the faulds an the rigs. They are no slaves. They are human beings that have the richt tae be treatit wae respect. Ye can only mistreat folk fer a while an then they fecht back. If ye dinnae gie them that respect, in the end they will disrespect ye and fin weys tae get back at ye. Wis it no the Lord Jesus Christ that said there were eleiven commandments and the eleiventh wis, "I command ye tae luv ane anither"?'

Meg's path led through a wood of silver birches that danced above her head and threw spangles of light across her old shoulders. 'We are nearly there laddie: the Warl's End.' She felt the frog get agitated. 'Dinnae loss yer heid, wee thing; at least no yet.' She patted her pocket. 'Och! Here we be.' She lifted the frog out of her pocket and held him in the palm of her left hand. 'Ye see, here is the Well at the Warld's End. Fer this is the end o yer auld warld, Alexander. Frae here yer fate hinges on ye.' Meg sat down on the stone at the well's edge, and looked into the spring boiling up three feet below, 'Doon there is yer new hame and yer hame it will be intil somebody agrees tae mairry ye. But, mair importantly, tae honour that agreement and tae show ye she cuid lue ye. Aye, an that's no aa. Ye see, the only wey ye can show yer love tae her is tae lose yer heid ower her; sae tae speak. Whit I mean is that unless she chaps aff yer heid, the spell remains.'

The frog's head moved vigorously from side to side as if saying, 'No!'

Meg ignored him and continued. 'Noo ye will ask yersel, "Hoo can I get someone tae agree tae mairry me? An even if I cuid, wuid they chap ma heid aff? An if they chap ma heid aff wuid I be free or deid?" Weel, Sandy. Dinnae think on juist whit I hae said this meenit, think on aa I hae said. Ye'll hae plenty o time.' Gently she dropped the frog into the well. 'I'll be seein ye!' she said before turning and striding purposefully away.

A mother was baking bannocks but had no milk, so instead she decided that, although not as tasty, water would do instead. She called for her daughter to fetch a bucket and go down to the Well at the World's End to get some – it was said that there the water was the sweetest anywhere. After the usual protest the lass found the wooden pail and wandered through the woods on her way to the well in the meadow beyond. It had been a long hot summer – the sun had come out in April and was still shining in August. The well was dry. Now Elsbeth, as her mother had called her, was a lass who could make the greatest drama out of the most minor of crises, so she fell to the ground and wailed. After noting that no one was there to pay her attention she stopped, dried her eyes and was just about to get up when a frog leaped out of the well. Such a fright did she get that she quite fell over. Lifting herself on to her left elbow, she looked at the creature, which looked back at her with what looked like a smile.

'Why are ye greetin?' asked the frog. Such a fright did Elsbeth get that she quite fell over again. The frog waited patiently until she had once more raised herself up on to her elbow. The frog cocked its head to the side, as if to say, 'Well, what's your answer?'

'I wis greetin because ma mither sent me tae the well fer watter, and there's nae watter.'

The frog gave her a long look then said, 'If ye want watter frae the well, ye'll hae tae mairry me.'

She laughed. 'Whit?'

'I said, the only wey I can gie ye watter frae the well is fer ye tae agree tae be ma wife.'

Elsbeth shrugged her shoulders, 'If that's whit it taks tae get watter then, aye, why no? I'll be yer wife.' She suppressed the desire to laugh, but merely grinned.

The frog leaped back into the well and immediately it began to fill with water. When it was deep enough, Elsbeth kneeled down, filled the bucket, stood up and walked away home without barely a thought for the frog, except that she did not take the vow seriously. She would have agreed to anything to get the water and besides, she thought, 'Wha cuild mairry a puddock?'

At home, her mother took the water and put it in a pot to heat. She made up dough with oatmeal, salt, water and butter and cooked it on her bannockstane. While still hot, they spread on butter and cheese and gorged themselves, even licking their fingers. Night was on them so they snuffed the candle and went to bed. Being a very small house, mother and daughter shared the one bedroom, which was also the sitting room and the dining room and the kitchen.

'Guid nicht, mither,' said Elsbeth.

'Guid nicht, lass,' said her mother.

Their heads had only touched the pillow when they heard a scratching at the door. This was followed shortly by the tiniest of knocks that in the daytime they would never have heard. Both listened and waited. Then came a wee gentle voice singing:

> *'O open the door, ma* hinnie, *ma* hert,   honey, heart
> *O open the door ma ain true luv;*
> *Remember the promise that ye an I made,*
> *Doon i the* meidae *whaur we twa met.'*   meadow

'Whit's that noise at the door?' asked the mother.

'Houts mither, it is naethin but a dirty auld puddock.'

'Open the door fer the puir wee thing,' said the mother.

'But it's a—'

'It's wan o God's craiturs,' said the mother, 'an I'll no hae ony dochter o mine mistreatin sic a thing.'

The daughter relented and opened the door. She watched as the frog hopped over to the fireplace and settled in the inglenook. It seemed to smile at her then began to sing again:

'O gie me ma supper, ma hinnie, ma hert,
O gie me my supper ma ain true luv;
Remember the promise that ye an I made,
Doon i the meidea where we twa met.'

'The wee thing maun be stervin,' said the mother. 'Gie it a wee bit supper, hen.'

'I'll dae nae such thing. Ye are encouragin it, mither.'

'He micht be a puddock, but he is a guest in ma hoose an as such is deservin o oor mense. Sae get him a wee bowl o brose.'

The daughter did as she was commanded, but not without gripes and grumbles.

'O tak me tae thy bed, ma hinnie, ma hert
O tak me tae thy bed, ma ain true luv;
Remember the promise that ye an I made
Doon i the meidae whaur we twa met.'

'I will dae nae sic thing,' said Elsbeth, deeply affronted.

'Did ye mak a promise tae the wee thing?'

Elsbeth didn't answer for a moment but could not lie to her mother. 'Aye,' she admitted.

'Then tak the wee thing tae yer bed. Whit herm wid it dae?'

The girl bent down and picked up the frog, wincing at the waxy feeling of its skin. It seemed to smile at her again as she climbed into bed.

'O pit me tae yer breist, ma hinnie, ma hert,
O pit me tae yer breist, ma ain true luv;
Remember the promise that ye an I made,
Doon i the meidae whaur we twa met.'

Elsbeth could not speak, so shocked was she as to what the frog was suggesting that she could only give a strangulated moan.

'Oh the wee thing must be cauld,' said her mother. 'It helpit ye in yer time o need, sae gie it a wee cuddle an keep it warm.'

Elsbeth lay stunned as the frog snuggled into her. But after a while both lay in peace, gently falling asleep. In her dreamy state she stroked the frog's amphibian skin, finding it strangely comforting.

As they all stirred in the morning, the puddock sang again:

'Noo fetch an aix *ma hinnie, ma hert,*   axe
Noo fetch an aix ma ain true luv;
Remember the promise that ye an I made,
Doon i the meidae whaur we twa met.'

Feeling more disposed to the frog, Elsbeth went out to the woodyard at the back of the house and fetched an axe.

'Noo chap aff ma heid ma hinnie, ma hert
Noo chap aff ma heid ma ain true luv;
Remember the promise that ye and I made,
Doon i the meidae whaur we twa met.'

Elsbeth stood looking down at the frog that was now on the floor, legs splayed and his head pulled forward in submission.

'I cannae dae that,' she said, though something in her seemed to say it was right to do.

Her mother, who was wise in the lore of life, said, 'Sometimes ye hae tae trust tae Providence. Whit else wid mak a puddock speak? Besides, it is the wee beastie's ain request.'

Elsbeth raised the axe and brought it down hard on the neck. She closed her eyes at the last instant not wishing to see her bloody handiwork. She turned away, dropped the axe and raised her left hand to her mouth as the sobs began. She felt a comforting hand on her shoulder, then a voice said,

'Turn aroon ma hinnie, ma hert,
Turn aroon ma ain true love
Remember the promise that ye an I made
Doon i the meidae whaur we twa met.'

Slightly bewildered, Elsbeth turned about to see a fine and handsome young man. Her bewilderment changed to wonder and joy as she recognised the smile.

The young man confided in them all that had gone before. How he had asked so many young maidens who had all understandably run off in fright. How he had pondered long and found the goodness within himself that lies at the heart of everyone. What had truly sealed it for him was the wisdom, the unquestioning kindness and the hospitality of Elsbeth's mother.

In time, Elsbeth and Alexander were married. The estate, which was nearly lost in his absence, was revived with the old factor reinstated. The old couple returned to their cottage to live out their days and Meg o the Moor's winter abode was renovated and rerooted. Alexander thereafter lived a good life until the end of his days. In all that time, he showed great love and, in return, was loved.

The Scottish Storytelling Centre is delighted to be associated with the *Folk Tales* series developed by The History Press. Its talented storytellers continue the Scottish tradition, revealing the regional riches of Scotland in these volumes. These include the different environments, languages and cultures encompassed in our big wee country. The Scottish Storytelling Centre provides a base and communications point for the national storytelling network, along with national networks for Traditional Music and Song and Traditions of Dance, all under the umbrella of TRACS (Traditional Arts and Culture Scotland). See www.scottishstorytellingcentre.co.uk for further information. The Traditional Arts community of Scotland is also delighted to be working with all the nations and regions of Great Britain and Ireland through the *Folk Tales* series.

Donald Smith
Director, Tracs
Traditional Arts and Culture Scotland